TABLOID BABY

KEVIN LYNCH

Fulton Books, Inc.
Meadville, PA

Published by Fulton Books 2020

ISBN 978-1-64654-982-5 (paperback)
ISBN 978-1-64952-620-5 (hardcover)
ISBN 978-1-64654-983-2 (digital)

Printed in the United States of America

To Mia, my sunshine and my purpose

Absolute truth is a very rare and dangerous commodity
in the context of professional journalism.
—Hunter S. Thompson

A NOTE TO
THE READER

MANY EVENTS IN THIS BOOK may bear similarity to some of the incidents that have occurred in my life. While I have pulled liberally from personal experience and described locations and people with subjective detail, rest assured the characters here are composites and this is a work of fiction.

MONDAY

"Look, Bernard…"

"Don't call me that."

"Bernie?"

"Don't call me that either."

"I'm not calling you Mr. McCaffrey."

"I'm not asking you to."

"What do you want me to call you?"

"The same thing everyone calls me."

"And what's that?"

"I've worked here for three years."

David Peril, the editor of the *Aspen Daily News*, leaned back in his chair and let out a condescending sigh. "Your byline reads Bernard McCaffrey," he said. "Why would I call you something different?"

"You hired me. I think we've had this conversation before."

"Do you know why you and Charlie are in my office?"

"You can just call me Mac."

Peril snapped his chair upright and slammed his palms on his desk. "Do you know why you're in my fucking office, Mac?"

The action didn't have the intended effect Peril was going for. Mac looked around the room. Charlie Montgomery, the Arts and Entertainment editor of the *Aspen Daily News*, was slouched in the chair next to him. It was 9:30 a.m. on a Monday, and he smelled like gin.

"I hope it's not to look at your nineties John Elway poster because that looks pretty dated. Isn't he the GM now?"

"Now you're a sports guy? I thought music was your beat."

"I've always been a sports guy."

"Then why do you work in A&E?" asked Peril.

"Because that's what I was hired to do."

"And what do you cover exactly?"

"You're the editor in chief. Or is that editor *and* chief? I can never remember. Either way, you read this paper, and you've admitted to seeing my byline. Why don't you tell me what I write about?"

"You cover live music. You write about local bands."

"Finally, a fan," said Mac. "You should let me read my work aloud sometime. It really pops when you hear the spoken word."

"Charlie said you want to get onto the news desk. He's said this a few times."

Mac looked at Charlie, still slouching. The fluorescent office lighting bounced off his forehead like a spotlight on a cue ball.

"Did he?"

"Are you interested in covering news?" David Peril asked.

"You mean like a town hall meeting? Doesn't Shane Benjamin cover those?" Mac looked at his flip-flops. Earlier, he had stepped in a puddle, and the cuffs of his jeans were still wet. He was wearing his yellow Hawaiian shirt today, the one with the blue parrots on it.

"No. Not a town hall meeting. This is still A&E, sorta. Maybe the Local section. I haven't decided."

"I'm not really sure what's being asked of me."

"They want to send you to Florida on a news story," Charlie said. "But it might go in the Arts section…or Local, apparently."

"But I cover live music. I write about local bands."

"Do you know who Conrad Harvey is?" Peril asked.

"Was," said Mac.

"What?"

"Was. Do I know who Conrad Harvey *was*. He died a couple of weeks ago. You sure you really read this newspaper, Chief? It was page-one news in this exact paper."

"Conrad Harvey has a daughter in Florida that's attending AA meetings," Peril said.

"Sweet."

"Mac, they want you to cover this as a news story," Charlie said.

"Why? Dead guy's daughter is an alcoholic? That's news?"

"Dead guy is worth a couple of hundred million dollars and only has one heir," Peril said. "Roxanne Harvey is about to become very rich, and apparently she's a drunk in Florida."

"Rich and drunk in Florida is one of my life goals," said Mac.

"This isn't a joke, Bernard."

"Don't call me Bernard, and yes, this is a joke. This is the *Aspen Daily News*. We're not the *New York Post*. Why do we suddenly want to cover a tabloid story in Florida about the drunk daughter of the poor man's Aaron Spelling? Are we the *National Enquirer* now?"

"Conrad Harvey has owned properties in Aspen for forty years. He was friends with Kurt and Goldie. Costner got married on his ranch. He's pumped a lot of money into the community," Peril said. "I thought you wanted to break into news."

"Just because something happens doesn't mean it's news."

"Everything that happens is news."

"Everything that happens isn't worth printing."

"We can beg to differ," Peril said.

"I ate some bad sushi last night and almost shit myself. Is that worth printing?"

"Conrad Harvey produced hit TV show after hit TV show for fifty years. He has one kid. Her mother, Suzette Cox, was a…"

"I know who Suzette Cox was, and I know she drank herself to death twenty-odd years ago. So what?

This is news? Her mother was B-list at best. She died in the fucking nineties."

"Mac, you're our A&E guy," Charlie reasoned.

"I cover live music."

"We're sending you to Florida."

"I write about local bands."

"You're going to Florida."

Mac looked around the room again and let out a conceding sigh.

"So I'm going to Florida?"

*****

Mac had definitely wanted to get onto the news desk. This was no secret in the newsroom. Why Peril wanted him out of town, however, was a little more surreptitious.

"Do you know Amy from the photo department?" Mac asked.

"Sure," Charlie replied as they walked down a narrow hallway back toward the newsroom. "The leggy broad that looks like she needs to eat a sandwich?"

"We went out a couple of weeks ago. We had some drinks and dinner. Ended up at J Bar."

"Okay, good. So she does eat after all."

"I saw Peril and his wife at the restaurant that night," said Mac. "He looked at us funny."

Charlie pumped some change into the vending machine and punched the button for a can of orange juice.

"Something was rotten. Didn't sit right," Mac continued. "So that night, in bed, Amy said something I found interesting."

"In bed? You had sex with the skinny broad from the photo desk?"

"That's not what's interesting."

"It is to me. My dick hasn't wiggled in two years, and I'm married."

"She said the last person she had in her bed before me was David Peril."

"What?"

"Peril was having an affair with Amy."

"The skinny photo chick?"

"Yes."

"Until when?"

"Until the night he saw us out together," said Mac. "I'm pretty sure he knows she told me, or at least he assumes she did."

"Why do you think that?"

"Because he sees us out having a good time, and then she immediately ended the affair."

"Did she give him a reason for ending things?" asked Charlie.

"I don't know what she said to him. I just know she stopped having sex with him after our night together. Said he's still calling her. She's been ghosting him. I guess I'm the bigger man."

Mac and Charlie sat down at their adjoined cubicles. Charlie reached into his desk and slid out a fifth of Tanqueray, mixing it in a coffee cup with the orange juice. "You fucked your boss's mistress. And now he's sending you to Florida."

"On a bullshit story, and on a beat I don't really cover."

Charlie choked down a sip of his cocktail and flinched a little.

"Are you really drinking that without ice? It's fucking Monday, Charlie."

"You did say you wanted to get on the news desk. This might help you get there."

"This isn't the kind of story we run. Since when do we break celebrity gossip? Where is he getting the budget for this? Sending me to Florida? Hotel and rental car. Per diem?"

"Beats me," Charlie said. "We haven't sent anyone on the road for a while." He switched on his computer and filtered through some files. "Here we go," he said, tapping the screen with his pen. "Here's the assignment file from Peril. Contact on this is a guy in Delray Beach. He goes by Leaky. He's the one that we got the tip from."

"Leaky? Why did he call us? We're not checkbook journalists. Why not call the *Enquirer*? This is celebrity gossip."

"Leaky's a Navajo. He grew up outside Durango where his half-sister works at the *Herald*. He told her about the Harvey girl. She tipped off Peril. She figured since Harvey had a connection to Aspen, we could run with it."

Mac leaned over Charlie's shoulder to get a closer look at the computer screen. "All of this is in the file already?"

"This story is gift wrapped," Charlie said. "This is easy, kid."

"How did Leaky get from the Reservation to Florida?"

"Says here he ended up there as part of a court-ordered rehab deal," Charlie said. "He saw the news about Conrad Harvey dying, and suddenly, the pretty girl in his AA meetings seemed topical. He called his sister."

Mac kept reading over Charlie's shoulder. "Peril put this all in an e-mail?"

Charlie spun his chair around. "When you get to Florida, contact this Leaky fella. Buy him dinner, lunch, whatever. Find out where the Harvey girl is attending the meetings. Snap some photos of her coming and going in and out of the meetings and hang some quotes on Leaky. The headline writes itself."

"'Alcoholics Anonymous, No Longer Anonymous'?"

"'Conrad Harvey Daughter in Rehab Following His Death.'"

"Mine reads better," Mac said.

"Stick to the story."

"Of course…always."

TUESDAY

People don't like to look at bare feet on airplanes, but that didn't stop Mac from wearing his flip-flops on the connecting flight from Denver to West Palm Beach. His Hawaiian shirts may seem obnoxious in Aspen, Mac thought, but the look would probably sell in Florida. He was still wearing the yellow one with the blue parrots. Maybe they were macaws. He didn't care. Either way, it passed the smell test earlier in the morning before he took himself to the airport.

After touching down in West Palm Beach and catching a shuttle to the car rental, Mac approached a woman behind the counter. She smelled like designer perfume and was wearing obnoxiously large hoop earrings.

"I have a reservation," Mac said. "It's either under McCaffrey or the *Aspen Daily News*."

The girl with the earrings punched some buttons. "Bernard McCaffrey?"

"Mac."

"Mac?"

"My father was Bernard. I'm Mac. Anyway, what kind of car do you have for me? Ferrari? Lamborghini? I look good in red, and I prefer Italian."

The girl with the earrings clicked some keys on her computer. "We have you marked down for an economy vehicle. Right now, it looks like we have you in a Honda Civic, to be exact." She looked up at Mac. "And I don't think it's red," she added.

"Can you upgrade that to a convertible at least? I'd like to experience why they call Florida the Sunshine State."

"The Honda Civic doesn't make a convertible."

"Yes. I know this. Do you have any convertibles at all?"

She punched some more buttons. "There is an upcharge, but we do have a Mustang convertible available."

"I'll take it. Just bill it to the *Aspen Daily News*. You should have that card on file."

"No problem, Mr. McCaffrey."

"Mac."

"No problem, Mac."

The girl with the earrings clicked her keyboard some more. Mac watched travelers wheeling their luggage around the terminal. The Palm Beach International Airport was pretty small, having only three terminals, but it was crowded for a Tuesday morning. Mac wasn't the only one wearing flip-flops.

"I'm going to Delray Beach. That's south of here, right?" he asked.

"Yes. Just take Southern Boulevard east. You can take 95 south or just stay on Southern until you hit A1A and then go south along the ocean."

"A1A? Like the Vanilla Ice song?"

"Or Ocean Boulevard. It's the same road."

"That sounds like a nice drive in a convertible."

"Absolutely. Where are you staying in Delray?"

Mac looked at his itinerary. "The Marriott."

"That's right there on the corner of A1A and Atlantic. You'll love it. Great location."

"What else can you tell me about Delray Beach?" he asked.

"If you're from Aspen, you should like it."

"Why? Do the slopes have fresh powder?"

"We have the sand, not the snow. But Delray has a bunch of high-end shopping and restaurants and lots of bars within walking distance of your hotel. It's affluent like Aspen, I would say. Classy perhaps."

"Affluent and classy? You mean snotty?"

"Is Aspen snotty?"

"Utterly."

"Well then, yes."

"How's the nightlife?"

"There's a bar on every block."

"Sounds like a great place for alcoholics."

"Rehab and recovery is big business down here," the girl with the earrings said. "Google it. There's been a lot of hoopla about corrupt halfway houses and health-insurance fraud."

"I can't think of a better place than beautiful, sunny South Florida and a town with a bar on every block to establish a drug and alcohol rehabilitation mecca."

"I know, right? I wouldn't want to be here if I had a drinking problem. Florida is a party place."

"Perpetual Spring Break."

The girl with the earrings smiled. "Exactly. But it's an industry here. Recovery. It's become the rehab capital of the United States. After the pharmaceutical companies got everyone hooked on oxycodone, the rehab industry exploded. It didn't take long for opportunists to find a way to profit. You should look into it. It's been all over the news. It was in the *New York Times*."

"The *New York Times*? Well, I guess it must be serious," Mac said. "That's all the news that's fit to print."

"It's big news."

"Apparently not at the paper I work for."

"What do you write about?" the girl with the earrings asked.

"Have you ever heard of Conrad Harvey?"

"The television producer? He just died, didn't he?"

"Did you know he had a daughter?"

"No."

"I cover live music. Local bands."

"Did Conrad Harvey produce music too?"

"Not that I'm aware of."

"Did his daughter?"

"The daughter you've never heard of? I don't think so, no."

"So what's the *Aspen Daily News* doing in South Florida?"

"I've been asking myself the same question." Mac took the keys and paperwork from the girl with the earrings. "Thanks for the upgrade," he said. "I like your earrings."

"Thanks. I like your shirt."

*****

"What's that noise?" Charlie said into the phone.

"Wind," Mac replied.

"Why is it so windy there?"

"I dunno, maybe it's monsoon season," Mac said while speeding past the million-dollar homes dotted along A1A with the top-down. He glanced at waves crashing along the beach to the east. Fluffy clouds floated above, looking like bleached cotton candy. The air was thick and salty. Mac accelerated. The Mustang had some kick.

"It sounds like you're in a wind tunnel. Or skydiving."

"You'd never catch me skydiving, Charlie. If you jump out of a perfectly good airplane for no reason, you deserve whatever happens."

"And that's your philosophy?"

"On that topic, yes."

"What's your philosophy on the matter at hand?"

"I still don't think it's newsworthy. Roxanne Harvey isn't news."

"Maybe not, but it beats covering The Chainsmokers again. They're playing at Belly Up this weekend. You said you wanted to start covering news, remember? You could be back here covering the same shitty scene."

"I'll say it again. This isn't news. But something did occur to me."

"Enlighten me."

"This story could have been handled in-house," said Mac. "All we had to do was outsource a local photog and interview this Leaky guy on the phone. We didn't need boots on the ground for this." He drop-shifted the Mustang and gassed it, ignoring the speed limit.

"Did you talk to Amy in Photo about your little work retreat?"

"My oral relationship with Amy has very little to do with actual conversation."

"I'm asking if you still think Peril shipped you out of town because you, uh…boinked his bimbo."

"Boinked his bimbo? Christ, Charlie, I don't think I want you editing my copy."

"Well, you know what I mean."

"I think it has something to do with it, yes, but something else occurred to me too."

"Continue, please."

"I'm the youngest guy in the newsroom by twenty years."

"So?"

"So Roxanne Harvey is thirty-one years old. I think Peril maybe wanted to send someone down here that's in her age group."

"That doesn't make a difference. You're not interviewing her. And besides, you said yourself someone could have handled this over the phone."

"What if we do interview her? That's the better story anyway. Why don't we try chatting her up?"

"That's not the assignment."

"Don't you think it adds a little journalistic integrity to contact the subject of the story? When *Rolling Stone* does a cover story, they usually interview who's actually on the cover, right?"

"Stop thinking like a music writer."

"I'm just thinking if we initiate contact with Roxanne, we might get a better piece."

"I take it you've seen what she looks like, right?"

"Roxanne Harvey? I've seen pictures."

"Are you sure she's not the *piece* you're talking about?"

"Why not get her for an interview?"

"Your job is to talk to Leaky first. If the story takes another turn, we'll navigate. Besides, do you really think she'd be impressed with your perpetual jeans and flip-flops look?"

"What's wrong with my flip-flops?"

"You look like a grungy surfer," said Charlie.

"This is coming from a guy who somehow looks like Humpty Dumpty both before *and* after his great fall."

"You look like if corduroy was a person."

"You look like you were dressed by a Walmart greeter."

"I'm sixty-six years old, kid. But at least I know how to dress myself."

"That will come in handy when incontinence sets in. You can change your own diapers."

"Just get to the hotel and contact Leaky."

*****

The girl with the earrings was right, Mac thought, as he rolled the Mustang into valet. The hotel was nice. Rising up five stories and across the street from the beach, the architecture boasted a Spanish-villa vibe. There was a pool across the street from the ocean, and Mac noticed blue beach umbrellas specked along the coast.

"Welcome to the Marriott Delray Beach," the valet said as Mac stepped out of the car.

"Thank you. If I need the car…"

"Just call the front desk, and it will be right here by the time you get to the lobby."

"Well, all right," Mac said, slipping a wad of crumpled singles in the valet's palm. "Sorry about the singles. I was drinking on the plane, and she had a hard time breaking a hundred."

"No problem, sir."

Mac grabbed his duffle bag from the passenger seat and pulled the second piece of luggage from the back seat. "Mac."

"Excuse me?"

"Call me Mac. I'm not *sir* or *mister*, anything. Just Mac." Mac looked the valet up and down. He was wearing a yellow vest and had cartoonish features. He looked like Pinocchio. Mac glanced at his name tag. "What's good for lunch around here, Bobby?"

"We have excellent fish tacos at the tiki bar, and at the lobby bar, I recommend the steak sandwich."

"Good to know. Where do the locals eat?"

"It's a little touristy, but there's a sports bar around the corner called Boston's."

"I don't think I could handle all those Yankee fans," Mac said.

There was an awkward moment of silence, and Bobby looked confused. "The upstairs is nice," he said. "Good view of the ocean."

Mac smiled. "Thanks, Bobby."

Mac wobbled his battered suitcase with the bent frame past the gift shop and up to the front desk. There was no line. The receptionist looked chipper and had frizzy hair.

"Checking in?"

"Yes, you should have a reservation from the *Aspen Daily News*. You can call me Mac."

"I have your reservation right here. Room 205."

"Room 205?"

"Yes, 205."

"Does the room have a patio?"

"No, sir. Just windows."

"Mac."

"Pardon?"

"Never mind. But let me ask you, which direction does room 205 face?"

"The window faces west."

"That's no good," said Mac. "While I am staying here at the lovely and tastefully adorned Marriott Hotel, I was hoping to be facing east. That's where the ocean is."

"There is an upcharge for an ocean view."

"The credit card you have on file is for the *Aspen Daily News*, is that right?"

"It certainly is."

"Put me on the top floor with an ocean view then, please. If you have something like that open, of course."

"We do. Room 500."

"With a patio?"

"With a patio."

"Great. Please don't charge the card until checkout, is that okay?"

"Absolutely. Let me finish this up…and here are your room keys. The pool is directly under your window. I'm sure you won't miss it." She handed the keys over.

"Even if I jump?"

"Excuse me?"

"You're excused. What time is happy hour?"

"The lobby bar has happy hour from five to seven. Tiki bar is three to eight."

"Anyway, I can get a few cold Heinekens sent up to the room? On ice?"

"That can be arranged."

"Fantastic. Just keep the tab open."

"Enjoy your stay."

"I do believe I will."

*****

A shower with clean towels made Mac feel like sovereign royalty. The coin-operated washer and dryer unit in his Aspen apartment complex was always out of order, and clean towels were a novelty. The hotel room was nice, the view nicer. Wrapped in a plush Marriott robe and sipping his second beer, Mac punched numbers into his phone. The phone rang twice before a muffled noise was produced from the other end of the line.

"Hello?" Mac asked.

"Huh?"

"Hello?"

"What?" the guy responded.

Mac took a moment to start over again. "I'm going to start talking now, and when I finish talking, then it's your turn. This is Mac with the *Aspen Daily News*. I am trying to reach Leaky."

"So?"

"So...is this Leaky?"

"Yes."

"Okay, great. Progress. You know why I'm calling?"

"My sister."

"Kind of. Your sister called the *Aspen Daily News* about Roxanne Harvey. Do you know her?"

"My sister?"

"No. Roxanne Harvey."

"No."

"You don't know Roxanne Harvey?"

"No."

"Let me start over," said Mac. "Did you see Roxanne Harvey at an Alcoholics Anonymous meeting?"

"Narcotics."

"Excuse me?"

"Narcotics Anonymous."

"You saw Roxanne Harvey at a Narcotics Anonymous meeting?"

"Yes," said Leaky.

"Have you spoken to her?"

"No."

"You saw her at how many meetings?"

"A few."

"Do you know what days you saw her at the meetings?"

"Tuesdays and Thursdays."

"And you saw her a few times?"

"Yes."

"How many is *a few*?"

"I don't know."

"More or less than five?"

"You ask a lot of questions," said Leaky, starting to sound annoyed.

"Yes, Leaky. I'm a reporter. We all ask a lot of questions. It's kind of what we do. Sometimes we even print your answers. Can you tell me where and what time she goes to the meetings?"

"Crossroads Club."

"In Delray Beach?"

"Yes."

"What time?"

"Eight."

"In the evening?"

"Yes."

"Can you meet me to talk about this? I mean, I'll talk. You can keep grunting."

"Sure."

"Do you want to meet me at Boston's?"

"No."

"Why not?"

"Place sucks."

"Can you suggest another place to meet?"

"O'Connor's."

"Is that in Delray Beach also?"

"Yes."

"Can we meet there tonight?"

"Yes."

"What time?"

"After work."

"What time is that?"

"Depends."

"On what?"

"What time the restaurant closes."

"You work in a restaurant in Delray Beach?"

"El Camino."

Mac sipped his Heineken. "That's Spanish for 'The Camino,' did you know that?"

"No."

"No hablas español?"

"No."

"I hope you're not the maître d'."

"Dishwasher."

"How about you call me when you finish work and I'll find this O'Connor's place, okay?"

"Okay."

"I'm going to hang up now, Leaky."

"Okay."

Mac hung up the phone, a little bit both confused and amused. Leaky didn't sound like he had much to say, but it was the only source on the story. He finished the beer in his hand and took the elevator back to the lobby. Mac slapped sunglasses on his face and stepped out into the Florida sunlight, placing one flip-flop in front of the other as he traipsed along the warm asphalt.

*****

Boston's on the beach in Delray looked like a Disney theme park dedicated to Boston sports teams. It smelled like lobster broth and inflatable pool rafts. *Leaky was right*, Mac thought while walking in. The place did suck.

"What can I get you?" the bartender asked.

"Clam chowder and a Heineken," Mac said, settling into a leather barstool.

He pulled out his cell phone and started sifting through photos of Roxanne Harvey from Google Images. Most of the photos were slightly dated, with the exception of the funeral photos. She was pretty, tall, and thin. Bleach blond, pixie cut, and pouty red lips. Long legs. Mac zoomed in on each photo, pinching his fingers in and out. She was certainly glamorous, even trendy. *She looked like Edie Sedgwick*, Mac thought to himself, the Andy Warhol muse that overdosed on barbiturates.

The bartender came back with Mac's soup and beer. "Is that Roxanne Harvey?" he asked, clearly staring at the photos.

Mac acted nonchalant. "Yeah. I heard she's a local girl," he said. He put his phone away.

"Not really. Her dad's estate is in Wellington. He had a big horse ranch up there. Polo team, I think. Something like that. Heard he just died, actually."

"Do you know her?"

"I used to tend bar in Lake Worth, and she came in on Wednesdays to sing karaoke and drink margaritas."

"She sings karaoke? What does she sing?"

"Blondie, the Ramones, and some other seventies stuff. Punk rock. She's got pipes. And she drinks her margaritas straight up, chilled with no ice. Salt rim. It's kind of a distinct drink order. She's hot."

"She drinks tequila? I thought she was an alcoholic."

The bartender leaned closer to Mac. "Listen, Betty Ford," he said. "Just because a lady has a few pops before singing 'Blitzkrieg Bop' in front of a bunch of tone-deaf retards doesn't make her an alcoholic."

"No, that's not what I meant. Someone told me she was in Alcoholics Anonymous. Or Narcotics Anonymous. Recovery, or whatever you call it."

The bartender shrugged. "I find that hard to believe," he said.

"Why's that? Don't alcoholics go to bars and sing karaoke?"

"I never really saw her overdo it. And I know plenty of alcoholics working in this business. Hell, a bunch of them work here. As for hard drugs, well, she looks pretty good if she's a junkie. She's not exactly aging like a meth addict. Not with that smile."

"Did she come into your bar alone?"

"No, she was usually with a friend of hers. Quiet brunette. Jane or Jamie or Jessica. Something like that. Name started with a J. That girl didn't drink. Maybe that's who you're thinking of. I assumed she was the designated driver, but who knows? Maybe she was the one in recovery."

Mac added some hot sauce to his clam chowder and dumped in some oyster crackers. "Do you know anything else about Jane or Jamie or Jessica?"

"Are you a stalker?"

"I'm just a guy eating some clam chowder."

"I really can't say much about the brunette. She was the quiet one."

The bartender wiped down the bar. The rag smelled like dishwater and ammonia.

"Soup is good, by the way, and sure, I'll have another beer," Mac said.

The bartender strolled off, and Mac finished his beer. He glanced outside across the street at the Atlantic Ocean. The palm trees were an unmistakable indication he wasn't back in Colorado. His Hawaiian shirts didn't seem so irreverent here by the ocean. The bartender came back with another round.

"Speaking of alcoholics…"

"Always a fun bar topic," the bartender interrupted.

"I was talking to a girl at the airport. She had fantastic earrings, by the way. Huge, big hoops. Anyway, she said this place is like a beacon for druggies and drunks. She said recovery is big business in South Florida, specifically Delray Beach."

"She wasn't lying," the bartender said. "Last I heard, there were about four hundred halfway houses in Delray city limits."

"Four hundred sounds like a lot. Why here?"

"Beats me. But you can bet every restaurant you go to around here has at least one busboy or bar back in treatment. They're everywhere. It's big money though, man. I know a guy who owned a couple of sober homes. He was getting five hundred dollars a week outta these kids, bunking two per bedroom. Two three-bedroom houses were pulling twenty-four grand a month. He was cleaning up. Last I heard, he moved to Costa Rica and runs a paddleboard rental now."

"I don't know if I'd want to come to Florida to dry out. I've had five beers, and my plane just landed a couple of hours ago."

"These are all rich kids. Poor people don't travel for rehabilitation. They go to local meetings and clog up diners. These are kids that started out snorting their Adderall in prep school and graduated to oxys before flunking out of college. The parents have too much pride to accept they're raising a fuck-up, so they send them off to an expensive rehab center. These kids finish a ninety-day stint and move into a sober house. Relapse and repeat. Sometimes they make it, mostly they don't."

"So is it drugs or alcohol or both?"

"Same shit. Narcotics anonymous, alcohol anonymous. Same program from what I gather. But what do I know? The opioid crisis definitely hit hard here. Seriously, though, this is bumming me out. Shouldn't talk about addiction at a bar. It's bad form. Like politics and religion."

"You wanna talk about Bill Buckner?"

The bartender shrugged. "I don't give a shit about the Red Sox, man, I just work here," he said.

*****

Mac finished his lunch and walked along Ocean Boulevard back to the hotel, taking in deep breaths of the salty air. The atmosphere was thick and wet here, not dry like Aspen. After picking up his Mustang from the valet, he pulled onto Atlantic Avenue and drove west. He punched "Crossroads Club" into the GPS on his cell phone. Leaky mentioned Roxanne had been attending meetings there on Tuesdays at eight. It was seven thirty, and he was only a couple of miles away.

The Crossroads Club was located next to an industrial park along a set of railroad tracks and adjacent to an interstate underpass. There were already several cars in the parking lot when Mac rolled in. He spotted a few people milling around outside the building entrance, and he didn't make eye contact with anyone when he drove by. He navigated the Mustang toward the back of the parking lot and backed into a position that offered a decent vantage point. The parking lot was well lit, which probably seemed like a good business decision when you considered the wayward nature of some of its patrons. Some of the overhead fluorescent lights flickered, casting dancing shadows on the blacktop. From his position, Mac could see the front entrance and the entire parking area. He slouched into his seat and waited.

A few minutes before eight, a white Maserati pulled into the parking lot with the radio cranked loud. Although he couldn't be certain, Mac thought it sounded like a Misfits song. The car parked near the entrance of the building, and all eyes fixed on Roxanne Harvey as she stepped out of the car. She was wearing leather pants and a tank top that hung off her shoulder in a purposeful way. She carried a large designer handbag and was wearing oversized white sunglasses on top of her head and bright red lipstick. She looked like a runway model, and she walked like one with extended, graceful strides.

Mac snapped a few photos with the Nikon he'd stolen from the photo department back at the *Aspen Daily News*. Roxanne approached the entrance, flicked a cigarette butt into the parking lot, and breezed into the building. The lighting worked good for the photos.

Immediately upon Roxanne's entrance, a blue Volkswagen entered the parking lot, catching Mac's attention. It approached much slower than the other vehicles. The windows were tinted, and Mac couldn't see inside. The car drove slowly past Roxanne's sports car and then to the opposite side of the parking lot and also backing into a parking space like what Mac had done. Mac waited. Nobody exited the vehicle.

At eight sharp, the remaining stragglers meandered into the building, but whoever was in the blue Volkswagen remained within the vehicle.

Maybe it was someone a little nervous to go to a meeting, Mac thought. Maybe the person had relapsed and was embarrassed to go inside. Whatever the situation, whoever was in the vehicle hadn't gotten out.

Mac slipped off his flip-flops and made himself comfortable. He plugged the digital camera into his laptop and scrolled through the photos he had just taken. There was no mistaking it: Roxanne Harvey was striking.

At 9:15, a sea of people flooded out of the Crossroads Club. Most were holding Styrofoam coffee cups, and nearly all of them instinctively ignited cigarettes. Some lingered and hung onto conversations while others quickly got into their cars and departed. Roxanne was one of the latter, jumping into her Maserati and speeding off.

Mac watched as the blue Volkswagen followed her out of the parking lot and onto Lake Ida Road. He followed the Volkswagen as it passed under the interstate heading east.

After a few blocks, it became clear whoever was in the Volkswagen was following the Harvey girl, though Mac had no idea why.

Maybe it was an old boyfriend, he thought. Maybe it was a drug dealer hoping to get her to relapse. Either way, he was still following both cars as they drove east and over a bridge to A1A.

They were driving north near a town called Ocean Ridge when Roxanne turned into the parking lot of a residential hotel. The sign out front read, "The Sun Dek Beach House," with the letter *c* intentionally left out. Roxanne parked outside, grabbed her oversized handbag, and disappeared out of view briefly, reappearing and walking up a concrete staircase. Mac circled the building and watched as Roxanne entered a corner unit on the second floor. Her doorway faced the pool. There was a patio off the back. The Volkswagen circled back, parked on a side street, and cut the headlights. Mac turned around and headed back south toward Delray Beach, a little more confused than he had been earlier.

*****

"Hi, Claire."

"Is this Mac?" said Claire over the phone. She had been working in Research even longer than Mac had been stuck in A&E. They had some history. Both disliked Peril and, for a time, enjoyed taking off each other's clothing.

"Yes, it is. I need you to run a tag for me," Mac said.

"What for?"

"Does it matter? It's work-related."

"Because every time we run a tag, we get hit with a database fee. Research desk needs editor approval for every lookup. Is Charlie your editor on this?"

"Yeah, he is. He'll approve it. It's a Florida tag, is that a problem?"

"Florida? What are you doing in Florida?"

"I'm not really sure yet. Are you ready for the tag?"

"Yeah, go ahead."

"Echo, foxtrot, delta, papa, six, seven."

He could hear Claire's fingers flicking the keyboard. "Blue 2010 Volkswagen Jetta. Does that sound right?"

"Yeah, that's it."

"It's registered to an Eli Stransky."

"Stransky. You got an age? Can you run him?"

There was a short pause as Claire continued scrolling her computer screen. "He's forty-four years old. Social security number was issued in New Jersey. He's got a Florida state private investigator license. And a concealed weapons permit. I can e-mail you his address if you want it."

"Yeah, do that. Anything else?"

"He's got a LinkedIn page. Says he works as a PI for Walker, Bisset and Turnhill."

"What's Walker, Bisset, and Turnhill?"

Mac could still hear her fingers tapping away. "Looks like a law firm in Palm Beach. The website says estate law."

"It's probably something to do with the will."

"What will? Again, what are you doing in Florida?"

"Wrestling alligators for hides."

"Oh?"

"Yeah, do you want a pair of boots?"

"No, thanks."

"A belt perhaps?"

"Very funny, Mac. Hey, did you fuck Amy in the photo department?"

"That's not a very ladylike question, now is it, Claire?"

"Well, I haven't seen you outside work for a while. Rumor has it that you've stopped messing with your girl here in the research department and you've moved onto the photo desk."

"You know a gentleman doesn't discuss such things."

"How would I know that? I don't know any gentlemen."

"You know me."

"My point exactly."

Mac mulled over the information he'd been given and jotted some notes down in his reporter's notebook. "So Eli Stransky, the private investigator, is working for the estate law firm of Walker, Bisset and Turnhill. And he's running surveillance on Roxanne Harvey."

"Who's Roxanne Harvey?"

"I'm just thinking out loud. Does this law firm have more than one office?"

"Website says Florida, New York, and France."

"France?"

"*Oui*. Bisset is French."

"Where's the Florida office?"

"Palm Beach."

"Can you send me the address along with the info on Stransky, please?"

"Of course."

"I miss your mouth, Claire."

"Fuck off, Mac."

"Atta girl."

*****

The first thing Mac noticed outside of O'Connor's Irish Pub was the kid in the adjacent alley barfing up what smelled like Jägermeister and Red Bull. The first thing he noticed inside was the gargantuan Navajo playing darts by himself.

"You must be Leaky," Mac said, walking up to the big man.

Thwap! A dart went whizzing into the dartboard.

"Can we talk about Roxanne now?"

Thwap! Another dart entered the cork with force. "Okay," Leaky said.

"Not big on the finesse aspect of the game, eh?" Mac said. "More of a power player, I see."

He slipped the big guy his business card from the *Aspen Daily News*. Leaky glanced at the card and crunched it into his pants pocket.

"I always thought darts was more wrist than shoulder," Mac said.

Leaky wasn't amused. "Drinks?" he muttered.

"Sure. I'll start a tab."

Mac ordered a couple of beers from the bar.

"Don't let the big fella overdo it," the bartender said, motioning to Leaky. "He tips okay, but he's a big bitch to carry out of here when he passes out."

Mac walked over to the wooden table where Leaky had posted up, a few feet from the bar and near the restroom. "I don't mean to get personal," he said as he sat down, "but should you really be drinking? I heard your vacation down here was court-mandated. Won't they throw you in jail if you fail a piss test?"

"Probably."

"Well, as long as you're not concerned…"

Mac took out his notebook and a pen. Leaky looked at the items suspiciously.

"This is all off the record, Leaky. Your name won't appear in the paper. But let me ask you something: what's your real name?"

"Leonard Lapahie."

"Leonard?"

"Lenny."

"Lenny? I guess that makes sense."

"Why?"

"You ever read any Steinbeck, Lenny?"

"No."

"Well, never mind then. Why do they call you Leaky?"

"I was a boxer. Navajo Nation champion."

"And Leaky Lapahie was your ring name?"

"I cut easy. I bleed. They called me Leaky."

"Excessive alcohol consumption does thin your blood, Leonard."

Leaky was still wearing his work clothes. "El Camino" was stitched onto his shirt. He smelled like dishwater and tacos.

"Shots," he muttered.

"You want to do shots?"

"Whiskey."

Mac ordered a couple of shots. Leaky took his immediately, chasing it with the remainder of his beer. He ordered another one by simply waving his hand at the bartender.

"I know you're not a very vocal guy, Leaky, but please tell me what you know about Roxanne Harvey."

"I got here from the reservation two months ago. Court ordered me to six months at a halfway house. I have to go to five meetings a week."

"How did you identify Roxanne?"

"Identify?"

"How did you know who she was?"

"I saw her on the news."

"After her father died?"

"Yeah."

"What was on TV, the funeral?"

"Yeah. She was on TV."

"And that's when you recognized her?"

"Uh-huh."

"Then what?"

"I called my sister. She works for the *Durango Herald*. I said a rich Hollywood guy died and his daughter was in my meetings. A few days later, you called me."

"Why did you call your sister about it?"

"I dunno," Leaky said, finishing off another beer. "We was just talking. She's my sister."

"Just casual conversation?"

"Yeah."

"Does Roxanne talk in the meetings? Does she share anything?"

"No."

"Someone told me they've seen her drinking at a karaoke bar. Have you ever seen her out drinking anywhere?"

"No."

"You said on the phone earlier that you've seen her at about four or five meetings, usually on Tuesdays and Thursdays. Is that correct?"

"Yeah."

"Are these Narcotics Anonymous meetings or Alcoholics Anonymous meetings?"

"Same shit."

"Not for a news article. I need facts. Maybe there's no difference in structure or format, but I need to know if Roxanne has an issue with the bottle or drugs."

"Why?"

"For one, alcohol is legal. If she's a hard-core junkie, the story gets a little more, I dunno, gritty, you could say."

Leaky just stared ahead blankly.

"So…"

"She goes to Narcotics Anonymous meetings. That's what I told my sister. NA, not AA. Court makes me go to both."

"Conrad Harvey dies, and his daughter is going to NA meetings. Does that sound interesting to you, Leaky?"

"She's pretty. She's rich. Isn't that what people read now? Kardashians, Hiltons? Famous people getting fucked up?"

"I suppose you're right."

"Let's do more shots."

"Okay."

Mac ordered a couple of more shots of whiskey and some beers. The bartender frowned.

"How was The Camino tonight, Leaky? You said you're a dishwasher there?"

"It's 'The Way.'"

"What's that?"

"*El Camino* is Spanish for 'The Way.' Not 'The Camino,' like you said on the phone before. I asked."

"No shit? Look at you fact-checking. Maybe you should be the journalist. How's it going over there? Are you climbing your way up the corporate ladder?"

"I'm just finishing my six months and going back to the reservation. I don't care for the humidity here. Or the dishwashing. Court is making me have a job too."

"What's your sister do at the *Herald*?"

"Reporter. Like you."

"Did she tell you she was calling the *Aspen Daily News*?"

"Mentioned she might. She knows a guy there."

"Yeah, my boss. He's a dick."

"So is my probation officer."

"I'll drink to that," Mac said, polishing off his Heineken.

"Let's do more shots," Leaky said.

Mac ordered a couple of more beers and shots and came back to the table. He made sure to order from a different bartender to avoid the stink eye.

"Roxanne shows up to these meetings in a flashy Italian sports car and looking like she just went shopping in Milan. She doesn't say anything in the meetings, and nobody talks to her?"

"The junkie hunters tried talking to her."

"What's a junkie hunter?"

"They troll the meetings, looking for people to relapse. They get kickbacks for getting new patients into a sober house. They have a deal worked out with the landlords."

"Is that legal?"

"Maybe."

"I've had a few people tell me the rehab and recovery scene down here is corrupt. Is that true?"

"Yeah."

"Aside from the junkie hunters?"

"It's an insurance scam."

"How so?"

"Drug test costs twenty-five bucks. Insurance gets billed fifteen hundred."

"I'm not sure I understand."

"A junkie hunter gets you into a sober home, and they drug test seven days a week and bill the insurance company ten grand. The sober house keeps the rest."

"The profits, you mean."

"Whatever. Let's do more shots."

"Wait…so rich kids get sent her for drug and alcohol rehabilitation. Once they start a twelve-step program and start going to meetings, so-called junkie hunters scavenge these meetings, trying to push them off the wagon?"

"Yeah."

"And then the junkie hunter pawns them off to another sober-house owner who then cheats the insurance companies on the cost of daily drug tests?"

"Pretty much."

"And nobody is doing anything about this? The insurance companies haven't picked up on it?"

"Guess not."

"How the fuck does Roxanne Harvey figure into this?"

"I dunno. How about those shots?"

WEDNESDAY

When Mac woke up on Wednesday morning, it felt like he had been gargling kitty litter. He was back in his hotel room, he knew that much. He looked down at the end of the bed. One flip-flop on his right foot was staring back at him. He wasn't certain where its partner was. Most of his clothes were still on, and there was an incessant buzzing in his head. Mac tried to sit up but thought twice about it. The buzzing was louder now. It wasn't in his head, it was his face. He lifted his hand to his cheek and felt his cell phone cemented to the side of his head with drool and slobber. The ringer was on vibrate. He could feel his teeth rattle. Mac didn't bother to check the caller ID. He peeled the phone off his face and pressed the button.

"I need an update." It was Charlie. "It's 10:30 a.m. out there. Peril is gonna be calling an editorial meeting, and I need an update on the Harvey girl."

Mac managed to sit up and look around. The room wasn't trashed, which was a relief. His eyes were burning.

"And what's this bullshit about you calling in tags for the research department? Whose tag did you run?" Charlie continued.

"Eli Stransky," Mac managed to say.

"Eli Stransky? Who the fuck is Eli Stransky?"

"He's a private investigator."

"And why do we care about him?"

Mac found his reporter's notebook on the nightstand. He flipped it open. For some reason, there was a sketch of Bart Simpson holding his penis that he definitely hadn't drawn. He squinted at the doodle and flipped the page.

"He works for Walker, Bisset and Turnhill."

"Who are Walker, Dipshit and Asshole?"

"Lawyers. Estate attorneys, to be exact."

"I'm sure any second now, you're gonna tell me what any of this has to do with Roxanne Harvey. Peril is gonna ask me."

"She has a tail," Mac said.

"A tail?"

"Yeah, and not a bushy one either. Although I haven't seen this Stransky guy. Maybe he's Persian."

"She's being followed? How do you know?"

"I saw it go down outside the meeting. I followed them both to where she's staying. Looks like some seasonal place. Temporary. Definitely not a Conrad Harvey property."

"Did you get the photos of her coming in and out of the meeting?"

"I'm no Annie Leibovitz, but yes, I got some photos. The lighting was good."

"E-mail them to me. That'll get Peril off my ass. And yours."

Mac was on his feet now. He grabbed a water bottle from the minifridge and finished it in one chug. He stepped onto the hotel-room patio and scanned over the Atlantic Ocean, inhaling the now-familiar salty air. "You don't care that she's being followed by a private investigator?"

Mac stretched out his arms and looked down at the pool.

"No, I don't," said Charlie. "That's not the story you're there to cover. The assignment is simple. Conrad Harvey's daughter is attending Alcoholics Anonymous meetings in Florida following his death."

"Narcotics Anonymous."

"Come again?"

"Narcotics Anonymous. She's not going to AA. She's going to NA."

"So we change that in the copy. It's the same story. Did you talk to this Leaky fella?"

"I did. He's a real windbag, that guy. Can't shut him up. Also drinks like Jim Morrison. Those Navajo sure enjoy the firewater."

"He verified he's seen Roxanne at meetings, and you have photos to back it up?"

"Yeah."

"So you're done. Write it up."

"I think there's more to it, Charlie. Do you know what a junkie hunter is?"

"Junkie hunter? What are you talking about? E-mail me the photos and start writing up some copy. Keep Leaky off the record, but hang some quotes on him as an anonymous source. Keep it under five hundred words and ditch the metaphors. This isn't a band review."

"I think I'm onto something here. You don't want me to at least find out why Roxanne is being followed?"

"Write it up, I said. I'll have the travel department arrange your return flight. I think you got it."

"You really think Peril wants me back in town so soon? I haven't spoken to Amy in Photo, but she's gonna get the photographs I'm sending. By now, she's bound to know Peril sent me on the road. Just let me stay a few more days and work this story some more."

"You have the story you were asked to get. Wrap it up."

"This is bullshit."

"This is journalism."

"The hell it is. This is putting on the condom and not fucking the prom queen. I have more leads to follow up on, Charlie. This story isn't finished. Something is going on here."

Mac was frustrated now, but his head was clearing up. He stepped back inside the hotel room and found the keys to the Mustang on the floor next to his missing flip-flop. He definitely hadn't driven, so that meant his car was still outside O'Connor's. He could hear Charlie huffing and puffing before taking a deep breath. He was talking, but Mac wasn't paying attention.

Finally, he heard, "I'm sorry, but you gotta do what the boss says if you want to keep working here and get on the news desk. Just do what Peril wants, and I'll get you more news stories. Maybe I can get you on the crime beat. But for Christ's sake, just send the photos and write the damn story."

Then the line went dead before Mac had a chance to retort.

*****

Mac quickly showered and got dressed. He slipped into his tattered jeans and flip-flops and pulled his orange Hawaiian shirt out of his travel bag, the one with the hibiscus flowers on it. He was still buttoning his shirt as he strolled out of the Marriott lobby and onto Atlantic Avenue.

Walking east, he traveled over a waterway and stopped for coffee before continuing on toward O'Connor's. Approaching an intersection by the train tracks, Mac noticed a cluster of police cruisers and yellow crime-scene tape. He approached an old lady walking her dog. It looked like a Pomeranian.

"Jaywalker?" Mac asked.

"Sort of. Somebody got hit by the train last night," the lady said.

"I hope they were insured."

"Health insurance isn't going to matter for that guy."

"I meant the train," Mac said. "It must have left a nasty dent."

He looked across the street and spotted his red Mustang parked in front of O'Connor's. The bar was open. He ducked inside.

"Excuse me," Mac said to the female bartender. He was hung over, but couldn't help noticing she had huge tits. He tried to not stare. "I was here last night, and I wanted to make sure I paid my tab. I also need a receipt if that's possible. I paid with a company credit card, and I need it for my expenses. The credit card said *Aspen Daily News* on it."

Before she could answer, a door behind the bar swung open, and the bartender from the previous evening appeared carrying three cases of Miller Light. He looked unfavorably at Mac. "Oh, hey, shit head. What did I tell you about letting that Indian drink too much?"

"Good morning, friend."

"That big fuck walked outta here last night and stumbled in front of the train. His body exploded like a goddamn water balloon, man."

"Leaky?"

"Leaking? No, *exploded*. Like a fucking juice box."

"The big guy, his name was Leaky. He's dead?"

"He's real dead, you idiot. I told you he couldn't handle his liquor. Oh, and expect a call from the cops. They found your business card in his pocket. They were just in here asking about you."

"They asked for a copy of your receipt as well," the girl said, handing Mac his own copy.

He looked at the receipt for twenty Heinekens and sixteen shots of Jameson: $258.00. He had scribbled in a 75-dollar tip, making the total 333.00 dollars.

"We drank all that?"

"You might have bought a round for the guys you played darts with, but it was mostly you and the big fella. The big *dead* fella."

"I played darts last night?" Mac asked.

"You threw some darts. You didn't hit the board."

"Did I leave with him? The big guy?"

"You stumbled out before him," the bartender said. "We had to kick him out right after that. He couldn't stand up."

Mac looked around the bar. It looked different in the daylight. It still smelled like shit though.

"I'm gonna suggest you fuck off and don't come back. Please, and thank you," the bartender said.

Mac walked back outside into the sunlight. He glanced back over at the train tracks about forty yards away. The yellow police tape was waving in the breeze. He walked to his Mustang and got inside. His phone rang. The caller ID said, "Delray Beach Police Department." He sent the call to voicemail.

*****

Mac drove to the Sun Dek where Roxanne Harvey was staying. Her Maserati was parked outside. He canvased the area for Stransky's Volkswagen but didn't see it. He parked his car within view of the Maserati and took out his phone then punched in some numbers.

A voice answered on the other end. "Walker, Bisset and Turnhill, can I help you?"

"I need to talk to the attorney handling the Conrad Harvey estate," Mac said.

"Conrad Harvey the television producer?"

"That would be the one, yes."

"Who is this?"

"This is Ray Chandler with the *Palm Beach Post*. We're writing a follow-up on the Conrad Harvey story. Has his estate been settled? Has it gone through probate?"

"You might want to check your facts, Mr. Chandler, but this office isn't handling Mr. Conrad's estate."

"Is Roxanne Harvey a client of your firm?"

"Under normal circumstances, that would fall under lawyer-client confidentiality, but in this case, I can tell you that no, Roxanne Harvey is not a client of ours."

"Oh, I'm sorry. I must have gotten my files mixed up. Is Mr. Stransky there?"

"Mr. Stransky doesn't keep an office here."

"Can you tell me why he's following Roxanne Harvey if this office isn't handling the Harvey estate?"

"Sir, I'm not privy to the daily routine of Mr. Stransky. But I think these questions are more suitable for Mr. Bisset. Would you like his voicemail?"

"Sure, that's fine."

She transferred the call, and Mac hung up before the machine picked up.

*****

While waiting for Roxanne to make an appearance, Mac flipped open his laptop and plugged in the Nikon. He uploaded the images of Roxanne and e-mailed them to the *Aspen Daily News* photo desk. An e-mail bounced back from Amy in the photo department.

"She's pretty," it read.

"No way. She's ugly," Mac wrote back. "Any idea why Peril sent me to Florida?"

"I dunno. Maybe to keep you out of my pants."

Mac saw Roxanne Harvey walking toward her car. She was wearing a yellow sarong and carrying a different oversized designer handbag. The LV initials stamped all over the bag hinted at its cost. She hopped in her Maserati and sped north on Ocean Boulevard. Mac slammed the laptop shut and pulled out slowly behind her.

Keeping a couple hundred yards between them, Mac meandered along, passing the mansions and villas along the coast. Roxanne turned into a parking lot adjacent to the Eau Palm Beach Resort. She parked her vehicle and walked up a pathway toward a boardwalk and past a sign that read, "Dune Deck Café."

From a distance, Mac watched Roxanne take a seat, her back to the bar and facing the ocean. The waitress smiled as she dropped off a menu, and

Roxanne smiled back. Mac waited a few minutes before walking into the narrow, open-air café. He tried to squeeze behind Roxanne's chair, deliberately bumping it with his hip.

"Oh, I'm sorry," he said.

Roxanne looked up. "That's okay," she said.

"Can I ask you a question?"

Roxanne Harvey looked up at Mac again, this time, tilting her head at a perfect angle. Her eyes were like sapphires. "Sure."

"I ate breakfast here this morning, and I dropped something of mine. It's gold and shiny. It looks like a sheriff's badge. Have you seen it?"

"It looks like a sheriff's badge or it *is* a sheriff's badge? Because I could imagine your boss being pretty pissed off if you lost your badge at the beach."

"I'm not a cop."

"So what are exactly we looking for?"

"My Congressional Medal of Honor."

Roxanne looked up with an element of mistrust. "You lost your Medal of Honor at the Dune Deck Café? You must be pretty careless."

"But also extremely brave."

"Has this bullshit worked for you before?" Roxanne turned back around.

"Can I start over? My name is Mac."

"Mac? As in McDonald's?"

"Kind of."

"If this segues into you referring to your dick as the Big Mac," Roxanne said, "I suggest you go back to the Medal of Honor story."

"My name is actually Bernard. But I go by Mac."

"Why not Bernie?"

"My last name is McCaffrey. People call me Mac."

Roxanne turned around again, this time taking a better look. "Your name is Bernie Mac?"

"I prefer just Mac. What's your name?"

"My name is just Roxanne, just Mac," she said.

"Your dad a big Sting fan?"

"I dunno, is your dad a big fan of *The Original Kings of Comedy*?"

"I don't think so. His name was Bernard McCaffrey too. I'm named after him."

"Was? Your father passed away?"

"Yeah. Two months ago," Mac said.

"I'm sorry for your loss. Do you want to sit down? I'm about to order lunch."

Mac took a seat next to Roxanne. She smelled like vanilla. *Probably her moisturizer*, he thought.

"What do you do around here, Mac? Besides try out cheap pickup lines at the Dune Deck?"

"I don't live around here," Mac said. "I'm here for work."

"What do you do?"

"I'm a newspaper reporter. I write for the *Aspen Daily News*."

"Are you from Aspen?"

"I live there. You ever been?"

"Yes, actually. A lot. My father had property there."

"Had?"

"Has. We still own the property, but my father recently passed as well."

"Well then, I, too, am sorry for your loss."

The waitress came over for the order. Roxanne ordered a Greek salad with no tomatoes. Mac ordered the steak sandwich.

"And you're working on a story here?" she said.

"Sort of."

"About what, if you don't mind me asking?"

"Junkie hunters," Mac said.

"Junkie hunters?"

"They're patient brokers that troll NA meetings, looking to bump people off the wagon and get them into a sober home. Then they bill insurance companies for piss tests. It's insurance fraud, basically. Probably sounds boring to you."

"I know what junkie hunters are, believe it or not. Why does this interest the readers of the *Aspen Daily News*? I thought that paper was all town hall meetings and artsy-fartsy bullshit."

"A rich family out there sent their teenage daughter to Delray Beach a few months ago for rehab. She finished ninety days in a reputable recovery center and then checked into a sober home. She got caught up with a patient broker who got her to relapse. He got her into a second sober home where they started bilking her parents' insurance company."

Mac flashed a look at the waitress. He smiled, and she noticed. "My steak sandwich is gonna need a Bloody Mary," he said. "Do you want one?"

"I'll have a margarita," Roxanne said. She kept her eyes on Mac. "Let me order. Continue with your story."

"Luckily, the parents back in Aspen knew their insurance broker on a personal level. Aspen is a small town. He tipped them off to the exorbitant insurance bills. They flew out here, snatched up their daughter, and brought her home. I think she checked into a rehab somewhere in Minnesota after that."

The waitress came by the table. "How is everything?"

"Bernie Mac here will have a Bloody Mary, and I'll have a margarita straight up, chilled, no ice, with salt, please."

"Coming right up."

"You have no idea how fascinating I find this," Roxanne said.

"You weren't interested in my Congressional Medal of Honor, but my junkie hunter story lights the fire? Maybe I'll lead with that next time."

"It's not that. My family has a rescue stable up in Wellington. We take in polo horses that are too old to compete."

"That's very noble. Not sure I understand what this has to do with my story though."

"One of the things we do with the horses is equine therapy with wayward youth. Are you familiar with equine therapy?"

"Sure. I've heard of it. Isn't that like mental health therapy with horses? There are some ranches out in Aspen that do that sorta thing."

"Exactly…The Sarlo Rescue Ranch is in Aspen. That's where my father got the idea. But about eighteen months ago, we hired a girl from Kentucky. Her name was Juliette."

The waitress came back with the drinks. Mac splashed a few dashes of Tabasco into his Bloody Mary before crunching into the celery stalk.

"Juliette originally came to us as a part of a rehab center in Delray Beach. They used to shuttle girls up to the ranch for equine therapy. She grew up around horses back home, and she was great with ours. After she finished six months in rehab, she moved onto our ranch. She was going to several meetings a week with Narcotics Anonymous. She was active in the program and dedicated to her recovery. She was great."

The waitress returned with their food. Roxanne forked a Kalamata olive and popped it in her mouth. Mac took a bite of his steak sandwich. The bread was soggy.

"Juliette lived with you?"

"She lived in the guest house by the stables. We gave her a job. She seemed happy," Roxanne said. "For a while, anyway."

"What happened?"

"She told us she met a guy in her NA meetings that was a pretty experienced scuba diver, I guess. He had a boat and stuff. Seemed legitimate enough. He started taking her out for scuba lessons. She went out and bought all the gear, mask, fins, the tanks, wet suit…everything. She started spending more time with this guy and less time with the horses. She was really into the scuba. They said in recovery, people tend to trade one addiction for another. In her case, scuba filled that void."

"This guy have a name?" Mac asked. "The scuba instructor?"

"She only called him Diver. She said that was his nickname. Diver. She said that's what everyone called him."

"A diver named Diver? How creative."

"She ended up relapsing," Roxanne continued. "She sold all of her new scuba gear for drug money. A few weeks later, we noticed some of the horse equipment was missing. A few saddles and some grooming equipment. She admitted to us that she had relapsed and was using again. She cried, admitted stealing and selling the stable equipment to feed her habit. We didn't want to kick her out or call the police. She felt awful. And guilty. It was hard to watch her come clean."

"She was probably embarrassed," Mac said.

"She was. I tried to keep an eye on her. I took her to karaoke a couple of times, tried to get her riding the horses again. But she was clearly still using. That's when she told me this guy Diver found her a sober house to live in. He convinced her she needed the structure of a sober residence and told her she could walk to meetings in Delray Beach. At that point, my father didn't want her at the house anyway."

"Did you ever see the sober house? Get an address?"

"No, but I know the general area. It's someplace in Delray Beach near Lake Ida Road and Congress Avenue."

"How do you know that?"

"She went to meetings at Crossroads Club. I dropped her off there a few times. She didn't have a car. I know she was walking to meetings."

"She still going to meetings?"

"No," Roxanne said. "Juliette is dead. She overdosed a couple of months ago."

"She died?"

"Yeah. I think the toxicology report said she had toxic levels of oxycodone and fentanyl in her system."

"That's sad. I'm sorry to hear it."

"I'm convinced this guy Diver got her hooked again," Roxanne said. "Does this sound like the story you're writing for the Aspen newspaper?"

"Kind of. I'm interested in any anecdotal information I can get. I'm just a little taken aback that I stumbled upon someone with so much information."

"There were over three hundred fatal drug overdoses in Palm Beach County last year. That's almost one a day. Unfortunately, Juliette's story isn't original. I just want to find this guy Diver and find out what he did to her. I want to know if he got her using again, and I want to know if he was getting kickbacks from the sober home Juliette was staying in. I want to make sure what happened to Juliette doesn't happen to anyone else."

"Did you go to the police?"

"They came to us. She still had our address listed as her primary residence. We were notified just after her parents were contacted back in Louisville."

"Did you tell the cops about Diver?"

"I did. They weren't interested. Said they never heard the name. Like I said, it's a common story down here. She was just another dead overdose victim at that point. Another statistic."

"So that's how it ends?"

"Hardly. I've been going to the same Narcotics Anonymous meetings myself to find this Diver guy," Roxanne said.

Mac finished his steak sandwich and pushed the plate forward. He took another crunch from the celery stalk garnish. "You've been going to Narcotics Anonymous meetings to find the guy you think is responsible for Juliette's relapse? I mean, you're not an addict yourself, are you?"

"I'm not an addict, no. I'm a social drinker, smoke a little pot from time to time, but I'm hardly what anyone would consider an addict. I'm going to meetings to get some information on Diver."

"If he's giving scuba lessons, he shouldn't be hard to find. What's your plan after you find him?"

"Like I said, I want to find out if he's the owner of the sober homes where Juliette was staying."

"You want to find out if he was a junkie hunter?"

"Exactly."

Roxanne crunched into her salad, forking the perfect balance of lettuce, feta, cheese, and olives.

"Is anybody helping you with this?"

"Funny you should ask that. My father was friends with Patrick Hanrahan. He's the Society and Lifestyles editor at the *Palm Beach Post*. He's an old-timer. He's been covering society in Palm Beach for forty years. You ever heard of him?"

"I can't say I have. Palm Beach high society isn't really my beat."

"I just figured since you're a journalist, you might have heard of him. He's a bit of a legend on Palm Beach island. He's interviewed every president since Nixon. They all come through Palm Beach on fundraisers. Hanrahan has spoken to all of them."

"Is he helping you with Juliette?"

"He's written about the opioid crisis and the sober house insurance scams in Delray Beach."

"Doesn't sound like a story a society editor would normally be interested in," Mac said.

"His niece was victimized by a junkie hunter. She managed to get clean and move out of state. Hanrahan was the only reporter at the *Palm Beach Post* covering the story back then. And since he was friends with my father, he said he'd look into it for me. It's not what he would normally cover, but he asked around."

"And?"

"Pat Hanrahan is seventy-five years old. I think. He lies about his age. He's only still at the *Post* for his social status, and they'll never fire him. But he doesn't have the same sort of nose for news that he used to."

"Nose for news? Listen to you, Bernstein."

"If you're looking for a good source for your story, I can introduce you to Hanrahan," Roxanne said. "He's a character. Thinks he's Truman Capote. He's a fabulous queen."

"Maybe I'll reach out to him," Mac said.

"I can arrange lunch, most likely. He likes to hang out around The Breakers."

"The Breakers?"

"It's a big hotel on the island. Fancy. Hanrahan pretty much has residency at the seafood bar there, drinking vodka martinis, eating cocktail onions, and rubbing elbows. It's his home base."

Mac watched as Roxanne finished her salad and took down the final sip of her margarita. She dabbed her pouty lips with a napkin, leaving a pink smudge.

"You want another round?" she asked.

"Why not?"

Mac motioned for the waitress. "Let me ask you something, Roxanne. What do you do?"

"What do you mean?"

"For a living. I'm a newspaper reporter. What do you do?"

"Are you really gonna make me say it?"

"Say what?"

"Let's see. Polo horses and a ranch in Wellington, property in Aspen, Dad was friends with the society editor at the *Palm Beach Post*. Maybe you're not such a great reporter, Mac."

"What's that supposed to mean?"

"It means maybe you're not so swift on the uptake."

"I assumed you have money, if that's what you mean. Your Louis Vuitton bag and Chanel sunglasses are worth more than my car. I can't even pronounce the name that's on your watch. I just wasn't sure if you worked for it."

"I don't exactly work for it."

"So what do you do?"

"You are going to make me say it, aren't you?"

"Say what?"

"I'm a little rich bitch, Mac. I was born into wealth, okay? It's not uncommon in Palm Beach. I've never needed a job."

"You don't think I see this in Aspen? At least your honesty is refreshing. It's important to know who you are. You don't work at all?"

"I oversee my father's estate. There's a lot of people on the payroll with the horses and everything, but we have good people running it. So I don't spend a lot of time up there. The estate runs itself at this point."

"Where did your family make its money, if you don't mind me asking?"

"My father was a television producer. He died recently, as I mentioned. Maybe you saw it on the news. His name was Conrad Harvey. My mom was Suzette Cox. She was a soap-opera actress."

Mac feigned surprise. "Your parents are Conrad Harvey and Suzette Cox? No wonder you don't work. I saw some stuff about your dad on TV after he died. They tossed out some numbers about his estate. Am I to assume you're the only living heir?"

"If you were to assume that, you would be correct. I'm an only child. My father's siblings are all long gone. My mother died in the nineties."

"Looks like lunch is on you," Mac said.

"I don't mind paying."

"I'm just kidding. We'll let the *Aspen Daily News* cover this one. You've given me some good information for my story, and I'm definitely interested in meeting your friend at the *Palm Beach Post*. Hanrahan, was it?"

"I'm going to a Narcotics Anonymous meeting tomorrow night to ask around again about Diver, if you want to come with me or meet me afterward. I'll be in Delray Beach. Is that where you're staying?"

"Yes, I'm staying at the Marriott on A1A."

"That's not far from my place. I'm in Ocean Ridge, just up the street from you."

Mac handed Roxanne his business card and took out his cell phone to enter her number. He had eight missed calls: four from the *Aspen Daily News* and four from the Delray Beach Police Department. Mac waved down the waitress to pay the tab, handing her his *Aspen Daily News* credit card. Roxanne gave him her phone number.

"I've got to make some calls for work, but I'm interested in meeting again," Mac said. "I think you might make a good source on my story."

"I'm just trying to get some closure for Juliette," Roxanne said.

"What was Juliette's last name anyway?"

"Morgan," Roxanne said. "Juliette Morgan."

*****

After paying the tab, Mac excused himself while Roxanne used the ladies' room. He walked back down the pathway toward the parking lot and noticed a familiar blue Volkswagen parked near Roxanne's car. He walked over and looked in the windows, but there was no one inside. Mac double-checked the license plate number. It was Stransky's car.

Mac jumped into his Mustang, pressed the button to put the top down, and sped out of the parking lot toward Delray Beach. He returned Charlie's phone call. He picked up on the first ring.

"What did you do?" he asked.

"About what?"

"The fucking cops are looking for you. They called the paper. Peril wants to know what's going on. The cops wouldn't tell him why they're looking for you. So I'm going to ask again, what did you do?"

"I cut the tags off my mattress at the hotel."

"Why are the cops looking for you, Mac?"

Charlie wasn't amused and clearly not up for playful banter.

"Leaky is dead."

"Leaky? The Navajo? How's he dead?"

"He got hit by a train."

"Hit by a train?"

"I guess you could say pulverized by a train? Demolished by a train? I know you don't like big words, Charlie. I'm trying to keep it AP style."

"What the fuck happened? He's dead?"

"Yes, dead. That's normally what happens when someone plays chicken with a freighter, Charlie. We met last night so I could interview him about the Harvey girl. We got drunk. I left and walked back to my hotel. He left and walked into a train."

"Jesus Christ."

"The cops found my business card in his pocket. They've been calling me. Sounds like they've been calling the paper too."

"Why haven't you called them back?"

Mac was reluctant to answer. "I was having lunch with Roxanne Harvey," he finally said.

There was silence on the other end of the phone.

"We can't run this story, Charlie. She's not an addict. She's only going to meetings to look for somebody that got her friend hooked on drugs. She's not a drunk, and she's not a druggie."

"You had lunch with her? As in you ate together, or you ate at the same restaurant?"

"We ate together. But don't worry, I paid for lunch. Well, actually the paper paid for lunch, but..."

"Have you lost your mind? Has the Sunshine State sunburned your brain? You killed the story!"

"I didn't kill the story, I was fact-checking. I can't write a story about Roxanne Harvey being a drug addict if she's not a drug addict."

"We have pictures of her coming out of a Narcotics Anonymous meeting. Pictures you took, by the way."

"I have a picture of you dressed up like Hillary Clinton at the Halloween party two years ago. That doesn't mean I'd write a story about you being a cross-dresser. Besides, I think I'm onto something. This whole rehab and recovery scene down here in Florida is fucked. There's a story here somewhere."

"That story is not for the *Aspen Daily News*. That's local news, Mac. That's a local story for Palm Beach, not Aspen. This is a Conrad Harvey story. Celebrity bullshit. Aspen, Colorado, Mac. We gave you the fucking headline."

"I think I am onto something, Charlie. Don't you care that Roxanne Harvey is being followed by a private investigator? There's something going on."

"We gave you the headline. The story wrote itself."

"Charlie…"

"I suggest you get back to the hotel and pack up your shit. I think Peril is going to reel you in."

"Give me a couple of days. I can still work this," Mac said.

"Go call the cops, Mac. I'll talk to Peril."

"You don't want me to find out why she's being followed?"

The phone went dead.

*****

Mac screeched into the valet station at the Marriott. The valet, Bobby, walked up to the car.

"Hey, man, the cops are looking for you," he said. "They said you're a reporter from Colorado. What are you writing about?"

"Underground, full-contact chess tournaments. It's a brutal sport," Mac said, walking past Bobby and into the hotel lobby. He entered the elevator and rode to the 5th floor, entered his room, and flopped on the bed. His phone rang immediately.

"This is Mac."

"Is this Bernard McCaffrey with the *Aspen Daily News*?" The voice sounded male and serious.

"This is Mac, yes, with the *Aspen Daily News*. Who is this?"

"This is Detective Dalton Deaver with the Delray Beach Police Department. We've been trying to reach you all morning."

"I'm sorry about that. I left my cell phone at the hotel."

"At the Marriott?"

"Yes. I heard you were looking for me here. How'd you know where I was staying?"

"I talked to your boss in Aspen."

"David Peril? He's a peach, right?"

"Not your biggest fan. He said you cover live music."

"Is there something I can help you with, Detective?"

"I'd prefer to talk in person. Can you meet me at the station?"

"I suppose."

"Do you know where the station is?"

"I'm sure I can find it. You gonna let me know what this is about?"

"It's about your dead drinking buddy from last night. Why don't you just meet me at the station in about an hour?"

"Okay, it was Detective Deaver?"

"Yeah."

"I'll see you in an hour."

Mac hung up the phone.

*****

Mac took another shower. The humidity and salty Florida air was lingering on him. He toweled off and buttoned up the same orange Hawaiian shirt from before, the one with the hibiscus flowers on it. He called down to valet and took the elevator to the lobby. He walked out into the sunshine and to his awaiting Mustang. He smiled at Bobby.

"You know where the police station is?"

"Take Atlantic, cross Swinton Avenue, and it's across from the tennis center. You'll see the cruisers out front. It's on the left-hand side."

"Thanks," Mac said, entering the vehicle and driving off.

Mac parked at the police department and entered the building. An angry middle-aged man was sitting at the desk. His badge said "Morris."

"I'm here to see Detective Deaver," Mac said.

"Is he expecting you?"

"Tell him it's Mac from the *Aspen Daily News*."

"Is he expecting you?"

"Why don't you call him and tell him I'm here, and he'll let you know if he's expecting me?"

"Why don't you tell me if he's expecting you or not?" said Morris.

"Do I look like the sorta guy that walks into police departments randomly asking to see someone?"

"No, you look like an asshole."

"And you don't look like you belong working the reception desk. What did you screw up to get desk duty? You forget to polish your badge...or your sergeant's dick?"

"I ran over an asshole in a Hawaiian shirt with my police cruiser." Morris picked up the phone. "There's a reporter here to see you," he barked.

He buzzed Mac into another section of the office where he was greeted by a second cop. The cop walked up and stuck his hand out. "Hello, I'm Detective Dalton Deaver. Come on into my office." He had a firm grip. *Typical cop*, Mac thought.

"Detective Dalton Deaver, huh? I guess that makes you triple D?"

"Yeah, never heard that before."

"Alliteration."

"I guess."

"Like Major, Major, Major."

"What's that mean?"

"From *Catch-22*."

"How's my name a *Catch-22*?"

"From the book...Major, Major, Major."

"There's a book called *Major, Major, Major*? What's that have to do with my name?"

"I think we may have gotten offtrack."

Deaver gave Mac an odd look. "Yeah, I'd say so. Just come have a seat."

Mac took a seat in Deaver's office and looked around. There was photograph of Deaver on a fishing boat called *The Takedown*. He was holding what looked like a barracuda. There were a few more photos of Deaver and some of his buddies at a Miami Heat game and hanging out on the same boat from the fishing photograph. There was another photograph of Deaver holding up a bowling trophy and some more egocentric nonsense.

Deaver noticed Mac looking at the pictures. "You a fisherman?"

"I've been fly-fishing back in Aspen. Never caught a barracuda before, though. I don't think they're native to Colorado."

"Probably not, but that's a kingfish, not a barracuda."

Mac nodded at the photographs. "Nice boat," he said.

"It's my brother's boat. *The Takedown*. He runs a charter."

Mac folded his legs, his flip-flop–clad foot about the same level as Deaver's desk. The cop looked at Mac's feet disapprovingly. Mac didn't give a shit.

"Do you know why we want to talk to you—McCaffrey, is it?"

"Mac is fine."

The cop didn't like looking at Mac's feet. "You know why you're here, Mac?"

"To talk about fishing?"

"No. Not to talk about fishing."

"Oh, I know. Maybe it's the dead Indian you mentioned on the phone."

"Bingo."

Mac rested his feet on the desk. He curled his toes for emphasis. "What do you want to know?" he asked.

"I want to know a few things. First, what are you doing all the way from Aspen here in Delray Beach?"

"Peril didn't tell you?"

"He said you normally cover live music. He said you were here working on a story and that Leonard Lapahie, the big dead Indian, was your source. He didn't tell me what you were writing about."

"I'm writing a story about tribal alcoholism. The Navajo have a long history of alcoholism, and Leaky was good subject matter. I'm sure you've seen his record."

"Leaky?"

"Leonard. His nickname was Leaky."

"Why did you fly all the way out here? You're a lot closer to Navajo Nation in Aspen than you are in Delray Beach."

"Leaky was here for court-mandated alcohol and drug rehabilitation."

"So what?"

"So court-mandated rehab in Delray Beach for a Navajo from Durango seems like an interesting story to me," Mac said.

"Why did you share a three-hundred-dollar bar tab with a known alcoholic? Is that some sort of Hunter Thompson thing?"

"His rehab was court-mandated. That doesn't mean he wanted to stop drinking. It just means the courts ordered him here."

"Do you know where Leaky was living?"

"I don't. Probably a sober home. I heard there's a lot of those around here."

"There's a few."

"He was working at a Mexican restaurant, maybe his employer knows where he was living."

"We know where he was working. Was he suicidal?"

"I wasn't really interviewing him about his mental state."

"I'd just like to know if Mr. Lapahie seemed suicidal the night you were with him. The train conductor didn't see him, so he can't tell if this guy jumped in front of the train or what. We want to find out if it was an accident or suicide. Or murder."

"Murder?"

"Maybe he was pushed."

"He was a big fella. It would probably take an even bigger fella to push that brick shit house into a moving train, drunk or not."

"Did you leave the bar together last night?"

"To be honest with you, Officer, I blacked out. I walked back to my hotel, but I don't remember doing so. Did you talk to the bartender from O'Connor's?"

"He said you left before Mr. Lapahie. About five minutes before."

"They have CCTV cameras there?"

"They do. We reviewed the video. You paid the tab and walked out. He left shortly afterwards."

"We didn't leave together?"

"Nope. You didn't. Watched you play darts for a while though. Obviously not your game."

"Have I done something wrong? Am I being charged with anything?"

"I'm just trying to find out how a guy you were drinking with all night ended up getting struck by a train five minutes after you walked out of the bar."

"I couldn't tell you."

"We're gonna get the toxicology results back. We already know he was drunk, but maybe the tox report will show if he was on any antidepressants or medications."

"That could be useful information."

Officer Deaver looked at Mac like he didn't trust him. He certainly didn't like looking at his feet. "You're here writing a story about tribal alcoholism by getting drunk with one of the tribe members? That doesn't sound like very responsible reporting, Mr. McCaffrey."

"I have unusual methods, what can I say? But if you want my opinion, I think Leaky got drunk and passed out on the train tracks. I have no personal indication from my brief communication with him that he was suicidal in any way. As for your murder conspiracy, it sounds like a reach. This doesn't strike me as a town with a high murder rate."

"Oh, you know a lot about Delray Beach?"

"I'm a quick study, and I ask a lot of questions."

"As I am sure you can appreciate, we don't like to leave any stones unturned."

"I can respect that," Mac said.

"Do me a favor. Don't leave town just yet. We're probably going to want to get a recorded statement once we finish the investigation and finalize the report. I can't do it now. We have to get a court reporter, and the local girl we have on payroll is out of town right now. I'd rather not outsource it. Do you think you can stick around through the weekend?"

"I can try and stay. I think my editor wants to pull me out of here."

"I can talk to him if you want."

"That's fine. I'll let him know. I love giving him good news."

"You should do some fishing while you're down here. Like I mentioned, my brother's got a charter boat. He'll take you out for a half day for a couple hundred bucks. You might as well get on the water while you're here. Good way to kill the afternoon."

"Do you have his card?"

Officer Deaver reached into his desk and slid a business card across. It said "Deaver Diving and Fishing."

"Fishing *and* diving?" Mac asked.

"He's a certified scuba instructor, too," Deaver said.

"Deaver the diver?"

"That's him," the cop said.

*****

Mac left the police station and called Charlie back at the office. "I can't leave town," he said.

"I'm going to put you on speakerphone. Peril is here."

"No, please don't."

Mac heard some mumbling between the two editors. It sounded like Charlie had cupped the office phone. Peril took the line.

"Mac," he barked.

"Hey, Chief."

"What's this bullshit about you not leaving town?"

"The cops need me to provide a recorded statement regarding this matter with Leaky."

"I just got off the phone with his sister in Durango, by the way. Obviously she's a little distraught."

"Having a loved one run over by a train may often lead to such feelings."

"Look, shit head, we don't have a story anymore, and we're wasting budget keeping you there. We're not going to interfere with a police investigation, but that doesn't mean I'm not pissed off about this."

"I told you it wasn't a story in the first place."

"If you had just submitted copy with the photographs without talking to Roxanne Harvey, we would have still had a story. You killed it. The photos were good, and you had the information from Leaky confirming she was going to meetings."

"You're upset because as a news reporter I found out something wasn't true and kept the *Aspen Daily News* from calling Roxanne Harvey an addict when, in fact, she isn't one? You're annoyed because I did my job? You're pissed because I kept the paper from printing lies?"

"Mac," Charlie butted in. "Tell Peril about the private investigator."

"What private investigator?" Peril asked.

"She has a tail. This guy Eli Stransky. He works for an estate attorney."

"Stransky? How do you know this?"

"Because I'm doing my fucking job," Mac said.

"Stop," Charlie ordered. "Look, David, let's keep him out there to find out why she's being followed. He's stuck there anyway until the cops get his statement. Let him see if it turns into something we can use. She's still Conrad Harvey's daughter."

"You don't know why she's being followed?"

"Not yet, but I have a feeling it has something to do with her father's will."

There was a pause on the other end of the line.

"Why would a PI be following her about the will? You said the name was Stransky?"

"I don't know why she's being followed, and I'm only assuming it has to do with the will because the guy works for an estate attorney."

"Stransky."

"Yeah, Eli. Eli Stransky," Mac said.

"What do you think?" Peril asked.

"I think we…"

"Not you, Mac. You can shut up for a second. I can't get you to wear shoes in the office, but can I get you to shut the fuck up for twenty seconds on the phone? Charlie," Peril said, "what do you think?"

"He's stuck there anyway. Let's see what he gets."

"You know I can hear this conversation," Mac said.

"Find out why she's being followed and report it back to Charlie. I don't see how this is going to fit into the paper, or the editorial lineup. But now you've got me curious, and the cops won't let you leave. Follow the rabbit."

"You got it," Mac said.

"Oh," Peril said. "Nice work on the photos. Maybe we can use them after all."

"Well, thanks for the kudos. I think that's a first," Mac said.

"Don't get used to it."

*****

Mac drove back to the Marriott, sat at the desk in his hotel room, and flipped open his laptop. He brought up the website for Deaver Diving and Fishing. According to the company bio, the owner was Officer Deaver's brother, Darrin Deaver. The company was registered and trademarked. Mac looked up the Palm Beach tax assessor's office and typed the name Darrin Deaver. According to the property records, Dalton and Darrin Deaver owned eight properties, all within Delray Beach city limits. Continuing the desktop investigation, Mac located a story in the *Palm Beach Post* written by Roxanne's contact, Patrick Hanrahan. The article referenced that sober homes in Delray Beach must register with the Department of Children and Family Services. Mac cross-referenced the Deaver brothers' property addresses with the registration list. Six of the properties were designated sober homes owned by Officer Dalton Deaver and his brother Darrin. Darrin the scuba diver. Darrin the diver.

Mac continued clicking the keys. He looked up the Palm Beach County Clerk's Office and ran the name Juliette Morgan. Six months ago, she'd been ticketed for open container and vagrancy at the beach. Mac looked at the address she provided on the ticket and then clicked back to the list of properties owned by the Deaver brothers. There was a match. Juliette had been living in a sober home owned by a Delray Beach Police officer. *Why*, Mac wondered, *did the Delray Beach Police Department own sober homes?*

He laid down and switched on the hotel television set. The Miami Heat were playing the Denver Nuggets. He was asleep before he saw the score.

THURSDAY

Mac woke up on Thursday morning to the telephone, which wasn't unusual. What was unfamiliar was the earsplitting ring exploding from the hotel phone instead of mild vibrations from his cell phone like he was accustomed to.

"That's a really obnoxious way to wake someone up," Mac barked into the phone.

"Hey, Bernie Mac."

Mac sat upright in his bed. He recognized the voice. "Clearly, this is someone who doesn't know me very well."

"Well, we did just meet."

"Is this about the kangaroo rental on Craigslist? Because I never said they were safe around children."

"It's Roxanne. Roxanne Harvey. We met yesterday."

"I gave you my cell phone number. Why are you calling the hotel phone?"

"Because I'm in the lobby."

Mac jumped out of bed. "The lobby of *this* hotel?"

"I'm not calling you from the Super 8."

"How'd you get my room number?

"I talked to Bobby when I went through valet. Did you notice that kid looks like Pinocchio? Anyway, he said you've got a suite here. Top floor with an ocean view? Very nice. I didn't realize the *Aspen Daily News* had such an impressive budget during these times of diminishing readership and an overall lack of interest in print journalism."

"Am I expected to stay below deck with the common folk? It's per diem. I think that means 'free' in Hebrew."

"Why don't you come below deck and get some breakfast with me by the pool?"

"Now?"

"Yes, usually breakfast is served in the morning, and I'm in the lobby of your hotel."

"I should shower first."

"I'll order you a Bloody Mary."

Mac showered, shaved, and dressed like it was a timed Olympic event. He picked out another Hawaiian shirt from his carry-on, the one with the flamingos on it. He jabbed his feet into his flip-flops and took the elevator to the lobby. He stopped at the glass sliding doors and saw Roxanne sitting at the bar. She was wearing a large white sun hat and laughing at something the bartender had said. She was wearing darker lipstick. Maybe you could call it maroon. Mac looked at his reflection in the window and wiped shaving cream off his earlobe. He casually walked outside and played it cool.

"Good morning," Mac said. "Thanks for the wake-up call."

"Aloha. Nice shirt."

"I have a thing for Hawaiian shirts."

"I see that. It's important to have a thing," Roxanne said. "But I'm not sure that's really a Hawaiian shirt."

"Actually, I've never been to Hawaii, and I'm pretty sure this came from Walmart."

"Flamingos don't live in Hawaii."

"Excuse me?"

"Flamingos aren't native to Hawaii. You might find them in a zoo, but they don't exist in the wild out there."

"Does Tommy Bahama know about this? I'm gonna have to let him know. Maybe write a strongly worded letter."

Mac took a seat next to Roxanne. She slid a Bloody Mary in front of him and held up a margarita.

"Cheers."

They clinked glasses. The bartender dropped some menus.

"I talked to Pat Hanrahan at the *Post* about you," said Roxanne. "He wants to meet you."

"Really? What did you tell him?"

"I said you were working on something in Delray about the sober homes. Told him you're with the Aspen paper. I think he knows your boss."

Mac pretended this didn't bother him.

"Pat's got a lot of friends in Aspen too. Remember, he's a society editor. The Palm Beachers love Aspen. Half of the people on the island have ski cabins out there."

"What did he have to say about the story I'm working on?"

"He said he'd love to help any way he can. Maybe we'll meet up with him. What are your plans today?"

"I hadn't thought that far ahead," said Mac.

"I saw that Mustang you're driving when you left yesterday. Maybe we should drop the top and take a drive up A1A into Palm Beach and see if Pat's around. He'll probably be shoveling oysters into his mouth at The Breakers around one."

"The Breakers?"

"Fancy hotel up north, remember? Do you have plans?"

Roxanne slid her right foot up her left leg. It probably meant nothing, but Mac noticed. Her toenail and fingernail polish matched her lipstick. Mac didn't know if that was a thing girls did.

"I don't have much planned for the day," he said.

Roxanne said, "I'm starving."

Mac looked at the menu and ordered the steak and eggs. Roxanne ordered chocolate chip pancakes with a side of fruit.

"You said yesterday that you and Juliette used to sing karaoke," Mac said. "You a big music fan?"

"Who isn't?"

"Any particular genre?"

"I like it all, but I'm a punk-rock girl mostly."

"California skater punk or seventies London and New York City?"

"Ramones, Sex Pistols…up to Misfits, Minor Threat, Fugazi."

"East Coast. You have good taste."

"I like West Coast too. Pennywise, NOFX."

Mac agreed. "Good choices," he said.

"I used to be in a punk band when I was a rebellious teenager. I was the singer in a little garage band. We sucked."

"You were in a garage band? That's sexy."

"We weren't very good."

"You were the singer?"

"Yeah, I sang. We were kids."

"What was the name of the band?"

Roxanne hesitated. "It really wasn't a big deal," she said.

"Come on," Mac said. "What was the name of your band?"

"Bashful Anus."

Mac choked a little on his drink. "Bashful Anus?"

Roxanne said nothing.

"Bashful Anus? You sang in a band called Bashful Anus? You have no idea how simultaneously sexy and appalling that is."

"We were kids. But I can sing the shit out of Blondie."

"Blondie isn't punk rock."

Roxanne gave Mac a playful backhand to the chest. "Blondie is punk as shit, dude!"

"I dunno, whenever I hear the song 'Call Me,' all I can think about is that old movie where Richard Gere plays a pimp."

"*American Gigolo*. He wasn't a pimp."

"Yeah, that's the one. Not very punk rock though."

"He wasn't a pimp."

"Whatever. You know the movie," Mac said.

"My father was friends with Richard Gere."

"Your father probably had a lot of famous friends."

"He did."

"How come you never got into the Hollywood scene? You could have been like Tori Spelling."

"Thank God I'm not," Roxanne said. "I know Tori…After my mother died, my father didn't want me acting or performing. If you don't know already, my mom had drug and alcohol problems. I was ten years old when she died. She's buried at Westwood Village Memorial Park Cemetery in Los Angeles, right near Burt Lancaster."

"Did her addiction have anything to do with your father starting the equine therapy and taking in girls like Juliette?"

"Of course it did. My father was a teetotaler after Mom died. He also decided to help young girls with drug and alcohol issues. He didn't want the publicity of opening a full-blown rehabilitation center because of his celebrity status, so he used the horses for equine therapy. He got to rescue old polo horses and run the therapy side of things on the ranch."

"But you grew up in Hollywood?"

"Until I was about twelve, then my father bought the ranches in Aspen and Wellington. I finished high school here."

"College?"

"No. I went into the Peace Corps for a couple of years. You're supposed to have a college education to get in, but my father pulled some strings. And when I say 'pulled some strings,' I mean he gave somebody a bunch of money."

"Peace Corps is pretty cool. Where'd you go?"

"I was in Africa. The second night I was there, a pride of lions stormed the village and ate all the goats and chickens. We spent the next six months building a fence."

"That sounds amazing."

"I loved it."

Roxanne finished her pancakes first and was picking at her fruit, spearing each piece of melon with a toothpick. She was struggling with the grapes as they rolled around the plate like marbles.

"What about you? How'd you get into journalism?" she asked.

"I grew up on back issues of *Rolling Stone*. My dad had an old Army trunk full of them. I read a lot of David Fricke at first, then I got into more of the news stuff like P. J. O'Rourke…"

"Hunter Thompson?"

"Well, yeah, what journalist *hasn't* gone through a gonzo phase? I interned at the *Village Voice* and wrote some band reviews when I was living in Brooklyn.

Got to hang out with Robert Christgau and caught a couple of shows with him. After I graduated college, I ended up in Denver writing for an alt-weekly called *Westword*. I eventually took the job in Aspen thinking I would start covering news, but I've been kind of pegged as an Arts and Entertainment guy. I cover bullshit."

"How did you end up on this story?"

"I pitched it," Mac lied. "The couple in Aspen that sent their daughter out here for rehab are friends with the publisher. I heard them talking in the newsroom on their way to lunch. I pitched the idea to kiss up to the publisher to try and get on the news desk."

"And they went for it?"

"I think the publisher wants to kiss up to the socialites who sent their daughter here. I think they were advertisers."

"Sounds like a lot of ass kissing."

"That's what modern journalism is. Lots of ass kissing," Mac said. "The entire industry is propelled by advertising dollars. Advertising dictates editorial content. It's kind of a disgrace, actually."

Roxanne stared out at the pool, no longer interested in the conversation. She changed the subject. "Do you want to go swimming?"

"I'm wearing jeans."

"Do you mind if I go swimming? That water looks amazing."

"No, I don't mind at all," Mac said.

Roxanne stood up and with one subtle move, slinked out of her sundress to reveal a white bikini and a flawless tan. Her skin didn't look like she had pores. She took off her hat and sunglasses and slipped into the pool, hardly breaking the surface of the water.

Mac looked the bartender, who was looking at Roxanne. Mac looked around the bar and pool. Everyone was ogling Roxanne like she was Phoebe Cates in *Fast Times at Ridgemont High*.

"There's no way that's your wife, dude, is it?" the bartender asked.

"I'm wearing a Hawaiian shirt and jeans that haven't been washed in six weeks. Do I look married to you?"

"I dunno, man," the bartender said, clearly not caring about any response to his question.

Mac continued to people-watch at the Marriott pool. Mostly tourists, he figured. Lots of pasty folks that didn't look like they got much sun. A few impressive golf tans and some obnoxious kids. He ordered a Heineken. He didn't care if it was ten thirty in the morning.

Mac noticed a middle-aged, single man over by the opposite end of the pool, sitting in a chaise. He was wearing dress pants and a pair of leather shoes. *Not really pool attire*, Mac thought to himself. Next to the chaise, resting on a towel, Mac noticed an impressive Nikon like his own, but with a zoom lens. Next to the camera looked like a digital voice recorder. Mac locked eyes with the middle-aged man, who tilted his head back and slipped under his panama hat.

Mac turned to the bartender. "Do you know Panama Jack over there?"

The bartender glanced over. "No," he said.

"Is he a hotel guest? Do you recognize him?"

The bartender took a longer look while stuffing bananas into a blender. "I don't think I've seen him before. Maybe he's waiting to check in. He's not wearing pool clothes."

"Where's his luggage?"

"Probably at the front desk."

Mac dropped his credit card on the bar. "Hold the tab open. I'll be right back."

He walked into the lobby and out to the valet station. He looked at the pegboard and the cluster of hanging key chains. In the middle, there was a large Volkswagen key fob with the unmistakable VW logo right in the middle of the black plastic key.

Bobby, the valet, hopped out of a Cadillac and walked toward the booth.

"Good morning. Did you talk to the police ye—"

"Did you park a blue Volkswagen?" Mac asked.

"Today?"

"Yes, today. I didn't mean have you *ever* parked a blue Volkswagen, Bobby. Maybe a guy wearing a panama hat?"

"What's a panama hat?"

"A fucking fedora-looking thing. Did you park a Volkswagen for a guy wearing a white hat? He might have been carrying a camera."

"Actually, I think I did. He came in after the pretty girl asked what room you were in. I have his key right here."

Mac walked back through the lobby and out to the pool. Roxanne was wrapped in a Marriott towel.

"Where'd you go, skipper? You go take a dump?"

Mac looked around the pool. The guy in the hat was gone. Mac walked to the fence and looked over and saw a blue Volkswagen heading south on A1A.

"Are you okay?" Roxanne asked.

"I'm fine. I thought I saw someone I knew."

"You're sure making friends fast down here," she said. Roxanne dried her blond pixie cut with the towel and shook it out.

"You wanna take that drive?" Mac asked.

"Do you have any pants that don't have holes in them? The Breakers is kind of upmarket, if you know what I mean. The flamingo shirt works though."

"I just have to go up to the room and change. You wanna come up?"

"Sure."

Mac picked up the tab, and he and Roxanne sauntered through the hotel and rode the elevator up to the 5th floor. Mac opened the door, and Roxanne beelined right for the balcony, tossing open the curtains and stepping into the salty air.

"Isn't this wonderful?" she said.

Mac rummaged through his carry-on and brought out a pair of wrinkled khaki golf pants, giving them a smell test. "Are the flip-flops okay?"

"Flip-flops are always okay in Florida. You can wear them to weddings and funerals."

"My kinda town," Mac said.

He dropped his jeans around his ankles and stepped out of the heap, then slid into the golf pants, completely unashamed to be dropping his drawers in front of Roxanne.

"We can swing by my place first, it's on the way," Roxanne said. "I need a quick shower and to redo my makeup."

"I think you look perfect," Mac said. "I don't think I'd be the first one to tell you that."

She smiled without blushing. "You'd be the first one with a Congressional Medal of Honor," she said.

"I should probably tell you something else."

"What's that?"

"I have a Purple Heart too."

She smiled again. "You're funny, Mac. I don't meet a lot of people I like."

"That's fair," Mac said. "I don't like a lot of people I meet."

*****

Mac and Roxanne drove about three miles north along the ocean, cruising in the Mustang with the top down. They passed beneath several canopies of banyan and palm trees before Roxanne directed him into the parking lot of the Sun Dek Beach House, where he had previously followed her.

The two-story building was U-shaped and situated on the corner of A1A and Inlet Cay Drive. There was a community swimming pool and a thatched tiki hut in the courtyard. Mac noticed a private sandy pathway between some palmetto trees leading out toward the beach.

Roxanne motioned with her arm, reaching across Mac's body. "Pull into my parking space," she directed him. "It's number 5."

They hopped out of the car, and Mac followed Roxanne up the concrete staircase, not hiding what he was staring at as her hips swiveled in front of him at eye level.

Mac looked over the railing at the pool. There was nobody around. "Is this a hotel?"

"Kind of. It's a seasonal rental. A residential hotel, I think they call it. The owners keep their horses on our ranch in Wellington. We don't charge them in exchange for this unit. I'm the only one that uses it. I've had it for years. The owners travel a lot. I think they're waiting for an offer from a developer to knock it down and build new condos."

Roxanne keyed the door and entered. Mac followed. The room was a standard boutique hotel room: a king-sized bed, a love seat with a coffee table, a large flat-screen TV, and a kitchenette. There was a patio off the back overlooking the intracoastal waterway.

"Quaint," he said.

"I haven't been staying in the big house since my father died," said Roxanne. "I'd rather be here on the beach. Besides, it's closer to Delray, and that's where I've been spending my time."

Mac looked at the paintings on the wall: Florida wildflowers, birds, and palm trees. There was a fake potted palm tree in the corner and a hammock swing seat next to it. The walls were painted sea-foam green.

Roxanne tossed her hat on the love seat and walked over to a small Bluetooth speaker and synced her phone.

"You want to listen to anything?"

Mac said, "You pick."

She turned on the music. Mac recognized it. British electro. *Mid-nineties*, he thought. He listened to the lyrics: *"Take me down, six underground...the ground beneath your feet. Laid out low, nothing to go. Nowhere, a way to meet."*

"Is this the Sneaker Pimps?"

"Yeah," Roxanne said, taking off her jewelry and kicking off her shoes.

"Not very punk rock."

"I don't always listen to punk rock," she said.

"I like it."

Mac continued listening, watching as Roxanne flitted around the room like Uma Thurman in *Pulp Fiction*.

"Calm me down...bring it around...too way high off your street."

"I'm going to take a shower," Roxanne announced before dropping her dress completely, still wearing the white bikini. She stepped into the bathroom and left the door slightly open. Mac could see her through the crack in the door. He kept listening to the music.

"Take me down…safe and sound, too strung out to sleep. Wear me out, scream and shout…I swear my time is never cheap."

Roxanne stripped off her bikini. Mac couldn't turn his eyes away. She slipped behind the shower curtain and out of view. The steam from the shower drifted into the living space.

"Mac?"

"Yeah, I'm out here."

"The door is open."

"Do you want me to close it?"

"No…I want you to come join me."

*****

An hour later, Mac and Roxanne lay naked in her bed, smoking a joint. Her head laid on his shoulder with her hand on his chest, feeling his heartbeat.

"You're pretty tan for a guy from Aspen," she said.

"Are you kidding me? I didn't see a tan line on your body. And believe me, I looked. I don't know how you manage that."

"I own a tanning bed, and I live in Florida. What's your secret?"

"It's Aspen. People spend time outdoors. I run, hike. I try and stay fit, which is hard when you're covering live music at night."

"Do you like writing for the *Aspen Daily News*?"

"Not particularly. My boss is a dick, and I'm stuck covering shitty cover bands playing to ski bums, townies and tourists. I like living in Aspen, that's about it. It's pretty. The air is still clean up there. The food is surprisingly good for a small town."

"Why are you so interested in this story? What's your interest in South-Florida sober living?

"I wasn't interested at first," Mac said. He was starting to believe his own lies. "The publisher wanted to gather some information for his advertiser friends as a favor. The newsroom back in Aspen is a bunch of old-timers. That's why I cover nightlife. These guys aren't exactly staying up late. There was no way they were gonna send anyone else. I've been asking to cover news, and they threw this at me. I was hoping this assignment could lead into a spot on the news desk and out of A&E."

"So you're not really interested in finding out why or how these patient brokers are preying on young addicts? The junkie hunter thing isn't your story?" she asked.

"I'm into it now," Mac said. "That's the story I'm writing. I didn't care on a personal level until yesterday and you told me about Juliette. I mean, she's dead. Maybe she's partly to blame for her own poor decisions, but it sounds to me like this Diver guy might be partly responsible. If I can help you find him, this story will be worth it to me both personally and professionally."

Roxanne rolled over and crushed out the joint. "It still sounds weird that the Aspen newspaper is laying out all this money for a story in Delray Beach."

"What do you mean?"

"A hotel suite and a convertible?"

"The only fiction writing I do is on my expense account," Mac said. "Speaking of weird, don't you feel a little weird smoking weed and drinking alcohol while simultaneously crashing NA meetings?"

"Maybe a little. Does that make me a liar?"

"Not by my standards, but as a member of the media, my bar is pretty low."

Mac's phone vibrated on the nightstand. He reached over and read the caller ID. It was the Delray Police Department. Roxanne noticed but didn't seem to care.

"I need to take this." He wrapped himself in a towel and stepped out on the patio and into the soggy ocean air. There was a neighbor watering his lawn. Mac waved, but the gesture went ignored.

He answered his phone. "This is Mac."

"Detective Deaver here, Mac. You got a second?"

"At least one for you, Triple D."

"We can't get a court recorder in here until Tuesday to get your statement. I'm not sure if you need to contact your boss back in Aspen and let him know, but I'm hoping to get you in here first thing Tuesday at 8 a.m. Can I get an oral agreement, or do I need to send a subpoena?"

"Normally, I wouldn't agree to anything oral with you, Detective, no offense, but I'll make an exception on this."

"Great, so I'll see you at the station on Tuesday at eight?"

"Yeah, I'll be the handsome guy with the blue eyes. Possibly hungover."

"And wearing an obnoxious shirt?"

"Sounds likely," Mac said.

"I'll see you Tuesday."

Mac hung up and dialed Charlie at the *Aspen Daily News*.

"Montgomery," he said, picking up his end.

"It's Mac."

There was no hesitation. "Peril killed the story," Charlie said.

"What?"

"Dead…killed…spiked. *No mas.*"

"Why?"

"You've got the *who* and *what*. I'm glad *why* is your next question. Maybe you're not the useless reporter Peril thinks you are."

"I can't leave until Tuesday night. The cops need my statement about the dead Indian."

"I'll let Peril know."

"Why did he kill the story? Yesterday, he told me to chase the rabbit. I still don't know why she's being followed."

Mac peeked in the window; Roxanne was getting dressed. It didn't look like she was eavesdropping.

"I guess he doesn't think it matters anymore. He changed his mind," Charlie said.

"So what the fuck am I doing here now?"

"You tell me."

"What does that mean?"

"You're still with the Harvey broad, aren't you?"

"Does it matter?"

"Not anymore, not for the spiked story. Maybe it matters to Amy on the photo desk."

"I doubt it."

"Maybe it matters to Claire in the research department."

"Since when did you get so absorbed in my social life, Charlie?"

"Kid, I'm just breaking balls. If I were you, I'd let it go and just enjoy your weekend in Florida. Maybe do some fishing."

"I think I might just do that," Mac said.

*****

The drive north on A1A, or Ocean Boulevard, was a mansion showcase. Roxanne pointed out Donald Trump's famed Mar-a-Lago resort as they traveled toward The Breakers to meet her contact at the *Palm Beach Post*, Patrick Hanrahan.

Mac was impressed with The Breakers as soon as they turned onto Breakers Row. The towering, opulent stone building oozed elegance and class. Mac circled a cast stone fountain adorned with carved nymphs and pulled into the valet station. "Looks like the Bellagio in Vegas."

"This hotel is older than the city of Las Vegas itself."

Mac took his valet ticket, locked arms with Roxanne, and was led into the hotel lobby.

"Pat's in the back at the seafood bar," Roxanne said. "I'm telling you now, he's an old queen. Don't be offended by anything he says."

Approaching the bar, Mac saw a tiny man in a cream-colored linen suit with a lemon-yellow bow tie and teal shirt. His hair looked like a puff of white cotton candy, and he smelled of Benson & Hedges and mothballs. Inching closer, Mac noticed the cotton-candy hair wasn't limited to his head but also stuck out of his ears like sheep's wool. He looked like a gay *Miami Vice*–era Don Johnson with an albino ferret wrapped around his head.

"Oh, *Roxxx-aaannnneeee*," the tiny man announced.

"Pat!" They air-kissed cheeks.

Hanrahan continued, "How are you holding up? I do miss your father as well, you know."

"I'm fine," Roxanne said. "The ranch is fine. The horses are cared for."

Hanrahan turned his attention to Mac. "This must be Bernard McCaffrey, visiting us all the way from the illustrious *Aspen Daily News*."

"Mac. People call me Mac. And nobody calls the *News* illustrious."

"I know your editor out there, Bernard. Yes, little Davie Peril, the nasal-voiced Jew from Cherry Creek. He's a little pee stain, that one. Please sit down and join me."

Mac and Roxanne took a seat. The bar itself was a fish tank. Mac watched a few clown fish scuttle beneath the glass under his elbows. The huge plate glass window behind the bar boasted a fantastic view of the ocean.

"That's a pretty apt description," Mac said. "How do you know Peril?"

"I've known Davie for many years. Ever since he arrived in Aspen actually. I have a lot of friends out that way. Would you care for a cocktail?"

Hanrahan waved to an Asian bartender that promptly dropped beverage napkins down in front of Mac and Roxanne. Mac ordered a Heineken. Roxanne ordered her usual funky margarita.

Hanrahan rubbed Mac's shoulder. "That's a lovely shirt, Bernard. Is that rayon?"

"I think it's Walmart."

"Aren't you cute? So Roxanne tells me you're working on a story about the sober homes in Delray Beach and the widespread insurance fraud, etcetera, etcetera…"

Mac said, "I am."

"What's your angle for the ostentatious Aspen readership?"

"I'm not sure yet. The publishers are interested. One of the advertisers' kids got conned by a patient broker. Now I'm trying to see if it connects to Roxanne's friend, Juliette. What about you? What gets a Palm Beach society editor interested in such a story?"

"A by-product of not fornicating with women is the inability to reproduce. Hence, I have no children. However, I am very close to my darling niece. A couple of years ago, Tiffany suffered a knee injury skiing in Aspen, which is a rather ironic twist in this saga. Anyhoo, after her surgery, dear Tiffany became hooked on painkillers. This led to some family strife, and my sister decided upon a rehabilitation center in Delray Beach."

"Why not up here on the island? I'm sure Palm Beach has some posh rehabs."

"Gossip, my dear. My sister is very social-conscious and didn't want word to leak that her daughter was a pill-popper in need of professional treatment."

"Fair enough."

Roxanne sipped her margarita, acting as if she'd heard this one before.

Hanrahan continued, "Upon finishing a ninety-day in-house treatment program, it was recommended Tiffany move into a halfway house for an additional ninety days and further treatment. All is well until Tiffany asks to move into a different halfway house she somehow found through someone she met at an NA meeting."

"Let me guess, he was a scuba instructor?"

"I am uncertain of this tidbit of information as Tiffany won't talk about it and has since kicked her habit and is now studying abroad at the London

College of Fashion. However, beforehand, when she checked into the second halfway house, she quickly relapsed, and my sister's insurance company suddenly became bombarded with exorbitant charges."

"For what?"

"For daily drug testing primarily. But Tiffany's addiction went from pills to needles very rapidly. It seems whoever got her into the second halfway house also introduced harder drugs. She wasn't using intravenously until she checked into that halfway house in Delray Beach."

Mac watched Roxanne casually lick the salt from her margarita glass. "What did you do after that?"

"I pulled a young reporter off the city desk and asked him to check it out. He worked the story for about two weeks and found out more of the same."

"More of the same?"

"It's a widespread epidemic, darling. These patient brokers or...what's the slang term?"

"Junkie hunters," Roxanne said.

"Yes, that's it, junkie hunters. So kitschy...I love it. Well, my intrepid young reporter started digging into this story and, rather suddenly, fled Palm Beach for an opportunity at the *Washington Post*. I don't know whom he had to fellate for that position, but needless to say, he's off the story."

Roxanne playfully toed Mac's leg from the adjacent barstool.

"What about you, Bernard? What information have you managed to drum up to give this story legs?"

Mac reached into his pocket and pulled out the business card reading *Deaver Diving and Fishing*. He placed the card on the bar and faced Roxanne.

"I'm sorry I didn't tell you about this earlier, but I think I know who Diver is," Mac said.

Roxanne picked up the business card.

"Who is Diver?" Hanrahan asked.

"He's the one that Juliette got caught up with," Roxanne said.

"I met a cop in Delray Beach. Detective Dalton Deaver. He gave me this card for his brother's charter and diving boat. His boat's named *The Takedown*. I saw a picture of it in Deaver's office."

"I know that boat," Roxanne said. "It's docked in Boynton Beach at the Boynton Harbor Marina. That's where a lot of the fishing boats rent slips. It's right around the corner from my place in Ocean Ridge."

"I dunno, something about the name Deaver. And his brother is a dive instructor. It sounded odd," Mac said. "Roxanne, you mentioned Juliette called that guy Diver. I took a gamble. I looked these guys up, Detective Deaver and his brother, Darrin."

"The alliteration is silly," Hanrahan said. "Parents can be so banal with alliterative names."

"The Deaver brothers own eight homes in Delray Beach. Six are zoned and registered as half-way houses," Mac continued. "Even if Darrin Deaver isn't the scuba instructor Juliette got mixed up with, we know a cop in Delray Beach is running halfway houses. At the very least, that's gotta be a conflict of interest. If not the *Aspen Daily News*, I imagine the *Palm Beach Post* could probably do something with this information."

Roxanne flipped the business card over a couple of times.

"Wow, Mac," she said. "I don't know what to say."

"I say we order another round," Hanrahan said. "Let's toast to this young man's journalistic instincts and the last bastion of the free press."

The bartender brought another round of drinks. Roxanne looked over at Mac. "Are you doing this for me?" she asked.

"I'm just working a story."

Hanrahan nudged Mac. "I don't think that's all you're working," he said.

*****

"So what now?" Roxanne asked as they piled into the red Mustang.

Mac stuffed a twenty into the palm of the valet. "I say we go check out this boat, *The Takedown*. You said it's docked in Boynton Beach? The address is on the business card."

"Yeah, I think it's docked outside of a tiki bar called Two Georges. In the Boynton Harbor Marina."

"Two Georges?"

"Yeah, it's across from another restaurant, The Banana Boat. There's a waterway between them, and charter boats line up there. It's a fisherman's dock."

"Banana Boat and Two Georges. We should have dragged Hanrahan along."

"Why's that?"

"They sound like a couple of gay bars," Mac said.

Roxanne shrugged. "I've never thought of it that way."

Mac navigated out of The Breakers' long driveway and turned south, back toward Delray Beach.

Roxanne changed the subject. "I probably would have slept with you even if you weren't working on this story," she said. "I don't want you to think I fucked you because I wanted anything from you."

Mac kept his eyes on the road. "You don't have to explain yourself. We're consenting adults."

"It's just that most of the guys that try and get in my pants want something. They want to have sex with Roxanne Harvey, or they're after money. You don't seem to be after any of that."

"That's because I'm not. You're sexy as hell, and you listen to punk rock. You had me at hello."

Roxanne smiled. The wind from the convertible caused her short blond locks to flutter and dance on top of her head.

"I like you, Bernie Mac," she said.

Rounding a corner on A1A and hitting a straightway, Mac glanced in the rearview mirror and noticed a familiar blue Volkswagen Jetta he'd become accustomed to seeing. He slowed down, almost to a stop, allowing the car to catch up. The front windshield was tinted, and Mac couldn't get a look at the driver.

"You know the speed limit is thirty-five along here," Roxanne said.

"I'm in no rush."

Mac kept his eyes on the rearview mirror. Before the Volkswagen could catch up completely, the driver quickly pulled off a side street and disappeared.

"Roxanne, do you know anyone that drives a blue Volkswagen Jetta?"

She wasn't really paying attention, staring lazily at the sky with her head tossed back and shades covering half of her face. "I don't know. Why?"

"Maybe an ex-boyfriend?"

"No, I don't think so."

"Do you know anyone from the meetings that drives a Jetta? You ever see a blue Jetta around your house or at the meetings?"

"Isn't that a common car?"

Mac said, "I guess it is."

"Nobody even really knows I've been living at the Sun Dek."

"Would anyone be following you?"

"Not that I know of. I have no idea why anyone would want to follow me."

Mac didn't know why either.

*****

Mac parked in the parking garage adjacent to the marina in Boynton Beach, just around the corner from Roxanne's rental. They walked along the dock toward Two Georges Waterfront Grille, passing a large blue-and-white drift fishing boat with *Sea Mist III* stenciled on the bow. The distinct stench of freshly caught fish lingered in the air. A couple of dozen smaller fishing boats lined the docks. Fishermen fileted their bounty, and tourists smiled eagerly, holding up their prize catches of the day.

Approaching an empty slip, Roxanne nodded in its direction.

"Right there," she said. "*The Takedown* docks there. They must be out on a charter right now."

Mac took a flier from within a narrow plastic mailbox. It was the same "Deaver Diving and Fishing" logo from the business card, along with rates and services and a photo of Darrin Deaver. Mac stuffed it into his pocket.

The bar at the end of the dock was large and rectangular with a cliché thatched tiki roof. A giant faux shark hung from the rafters. The waitresses were all wearing tight shorts. They took a seat at the bar and ordered their usual, her confusing margarita and a cold Heineken for him. They waited.

A solo acoustic guitar player pumped out a few Jimmy Buffet tunes as boats drifted in and out of the channel. A breeze blew off the intracoastal waterway.

About an hour later, *The Takedown* came into view rounding into the slip area from the north.

Mac took another look at the flier in his pocket and the photograph on the boat. "Here they come," he said. "That's Deaver's boat."

The boat itself was nothing remarkable and appeared to be a standard, run-of-the-mill Florida fishing boat with two outboard motors and a fishing tower. The port side of the boat housed about a half-dozen scuba tanks, while starboard contained the fishing gear. There was a red stripe along the boat, and *The Takedown* was stenciled in large block letters across the stern.

Mac and Roxanne watched as the boat docked and two crew members helped the passengers depart. A pretty blonde took Darrin Deaver's hand and stepped off the boat.

"I know her," Roxanne said. "I know that girl."

"From the NA meetings?"

"Yeah, her name is Maggie. She's from somewhere in New England. I forget where. Connecticut or Rhode Island. I've seen her a few times."

"Do you know her last name?"

"No. I think that's part of the whole *anonymous* thing. You know, anonymity."

Mac said, "Right."

He motioned for the bar tab and slipped his *Aspen Daily News* credit card to one of the waitresses in the Daisy Dukes. They watched as the boat's passengers all slowly departed the area. Maggie lingered and spoke with Darrin Deaver for a moment before giving him a kiss and walking off down the dock with another girl. He playfully slapped her ass as she turned around. She spun like a flirty schoolgirl.

"And there you have it," Roxanne said. "That's his girl."

"Come on, let's go."

"Where are we going?"

"We're gonna follow her. Let's see if she's living in one of the Deaver sober homes. I have the addresses."

Mac and Roxanne followed Maggie and the other girl as they entered the parking garage at the east end of the docks. Mac took the stairs to the third floor, taking two steps at a time, while Roxanne waited at the garage entrance. Mac was out of the garage quickly and scooped up Roxanne.

"Follow the Acura," said Roxanne. "She's in that red car. Her friend is driving."

She closed the car door. "This is exciting," she said. "Is this what you do in Aspen?"

"Not so much," Mac said.

"What happens when they get where they're going?"

"Let's see where they're going first. A journalist once told me our actions are decided by the actions of others."

Mac followed as Maggie and her friend drove into Delray Beach city limits and into an adjacent neighborhood off of Swinton Avenue.

"I love this car, but it's not exactly inconspicuous," Mac said.

The car pulled in front of a ranch-style house with no garage. There were four other cars in the driveway and in front of the house. Mac noticed none of them had Florida license plates. Both girls hopped out of the car and walked into the house. Mac drove by and clocked the address. He then turned around and parked down the street behind a parked SUV.

"Do you know where we are?" Mac asked. "Do you know this neighborhood?"

"We're really close to the Crossroads Club," Roxanne said. "That's where the local NA meetings are."

Mac pressed the button to close the ragtop on the Mustang.

"What now?" Roxanne asked.

"We're gonna wait."

"For Maggie?"

"For anyone except Maggie."

"Why?"

"You saw Deaver slap her ass. That's his honey-pot. There's no way she turns on him. She'll go right back and tell him somebody's been asking about him. He'll tell his brother. The last thing I need is the Delray Police Department to know what I'm looking into. My plan? I say we look for the most strung-out girl we see leaving that house and hit her up. Find out how she ended up in this specific halfway house."

"How do you know it's a halfway house?"

"Not one of those cars in the driveway or on the lawn have Florida tags, and they're all from different states. The blue Honda has Rhode Island plates. I'm willing to bet that's Maggie's car."

"How long are we going to sit here?"

"I have no idea. I can take you home if you want. Or you can hang around my hotel room. I'll give you my key."

"Hell no. I'm having fun."

"Not bad for a first date, eh?"

"I feel like our first date has been going on for a while now."

Mac smiled and reclined his seat. "We have time to talk," he said. "Tell me about your mom."

"What do you want to know?"

"I dunno, really. I mean, I never watched daytime television, but I know the name Suzette Cox just as well as I know the name Susan Lucci. And obviously, I've heard of your father."

"I was ten when she died. I was little, but I remember her. We had fun. I used to brush her hair, and she'd bring me on the set once in a while," Roxanne said.

"Were you old enough to understand what was going on?"

"Definitely. My mom would go on benders and run around the house naked. She'd prance nude in front of the gardeners and the kitchen staff. I would chase her around with a robe and try and cover her up."

"That sounds unpleasant."

"Probably not for the gardeners. My mom was hot."

"I've seen pictures," Mac said.

"It wasn't easy, but I had no frame of reference. It was Hollywood in the nineties. Cocaine was passé, ecstasy was just hitting the scene, and my mom was a party girl. My dad was almost forty years older than her. I mean, think about that age gap in reality and not Hollywood."

"Were they in love?"

"My parents? Maybe. I doubt it. She married him for money and stability, and he wanted a trophy wife. I'm not fucking stupid."

"Were you close with your father?"

"He was more like my grandfather."

"In what way?"

"It's hard to explain," Roxanne said. "He was never very affectionate with me. He never hugged me. I mean, he told me he loved me, and he obviously provided a lifestyle most people can't fathom. But something just seemed weird. I didn't have any siblings, so it wasn't like he played favorites or anything like that. He was just distant. Supportive and gentle, but distant."

They sat in silence for a few minutes until the front door of the sober house opened and a young girl with a ponytail and wearing a Green Day T-shirt bounded out and started walking down the sidewalk toward Lake Ida Road.

"That's our girl," Mac said. He roared the Mustang to life. "Let's see what she has to say."

Mac followed behind, giving a couple of blocks of distance. She didn't look back over her shoulder, but she walked at a decent clip.

Mac asked, "I wonder where she's going."

Roxanne looked at her watch. "She's heading toward the Crossroads Club. She might be going to a meeting."

"Let's stop her outside."

Mac drove around the block and passed the girl on a parallel cross street, trying his best to keep the car out of sight. He drove under Interstate 95 and pulled into the Crossroads Club. They could see the girl still walking in the same direction. Mac parked the car.

"I think it's your turn," he said.

Roxanne got out of the car and lit a cigarette. She walked toward the front of the building and stopped short of the entrance. The girl approached the doorway, and Mac watched as Roxanne held out an open pack of cigarettes. The girl smiled and pulled a cigarette from Roxanne's extended pack and lit up. The two girls were chatting.

The girl waved her hands in the air emphatically, as if she was telling a big story. Roxanne smiled and nodded, and the girl kept talking.

After a few moments, Roxanne turned over and motioned toward the Mustang. The girl nodded again. They walked back toward the car, and Roxanne opened the door.

"Sadie here said she wants to get a cup of coffee with us. You cool with that?"

Mac pushed the seat back. "Hop on in," he said.

*****

Mac drove the trio to a Starbucks on the corner of Atlantic Avenue and US 1. The coffee shop was located within a strange little Antique Mall. Coffee and crystal trinkets seemed like an odd combination. Mac ordered a triple espresso while Roxanne and Sadie both ordered some bullshit hoity-toity coffee abominations. They took seats by the window.

"Okay, so this is how it works," Sadie began. "A lot of the people here for recovery are still using. It's not like you check into a rehab and suddenly you're no longer an addict. Relapse is part of recovery, at least that's what they keep reminding us in meetings. Because we're all from out of state, we don't have dealers here. We have to try and score on the street. That's how you get busted. Most of us have priors back home, and one of the reasons a lot of us are here is because our lawyers got us rehab instead of jail time."

Sadie blew across the top of her coffee cup and kept talking. She was chewing gum obnoxiously, snapping the pink wad and blowing bubbles. Mac wondered how it paired with her nine-dollar mocha latte, whipped cream, and caramel drizzle concoction.

"Delray PD busts one of the girls and offers an ultimatum," she continued. "Leave your halfway house and check into one of the houses they suggest, and they won't take you to jail for possession."

"They give you a list of halfway houses?" Mac asked.

"Yeah."

"Doesn't that seem weird to you, Sadie?" Mac asked. "The cops pick you up on a possession charge and then order you to check into a halfway house?"

"A halfway house of their choosing," Roxanne added.

"They give you a list," Sadie said. "They tell you which ones have beds available."

Mac asked, "Do you know all the addresses? Of all the halfway houses?"

Sadie sipped her coffee. "I know what streets they're on, not every house number. You two ask a lot of fucking questions. What's going on?"

Mac took out his phone and opened a screen. He showed a list of addresses to Sadie. "Are these the same street names?"

"Yeah, that looks like them," she said.

"But if you're using, wouldn't you get kicked out of your current halfway house anyway?" Roxanne asked.

"Most houses have a designated pisser. The homeowners don't give a shit if we're getting high. They just want clean piss to send to the lab every day so they can bill our parents' insurance companies."

Mac tried to wrap his head around what Sadie was telling him. "Let me get this straight again. Delray PD picks you up for possession. They find out you're down here in recovery and essentially force you into a specific halfway house…or arrest you?"

"Yeah, that about sums it up. Who are you guys anyway?"

"Do you know the name Juliette Morgan?" Roxanne asked.

"I think so. Didn't she OD a couple of months ago?"

"She did," Roxanne said. "She was my friend."

"I heard she used to date my landlord. The guy that owns my halfway house. Now he's dating my roommate."

"Darrin Deaver?"

"Yeah, Diver. We all call him Diver on account of his being a scuba guy and all."

"And you know his brother's a cop, right?" Mac asked.

"Yeah. He's the guy that busted me on possession."

"None of this sounds like a shakedown to you, Sadie?" Roxanne asked.

"Of course, it does. But what's my other option? Go to jail? Fuck that."

"So that's the whole con? Check into this sober home or go to jail?"

"There's another scam too." Sadie paused for another sip of coffee. "Sometimes the girls aren't using at all, and they're taking recovery serious. After all, not every single sober house down here is, I dunno how to say it...crooked? There are people taking recovery pretty seriously. So to get those girls, they try and get them to relapse and get kicked out of their living situation. Then Darrin tells them he's got a bed and checks them in, telling them he doesn't care if she's still getting high. Like I said, they've got designated pissers. They just need our insurance. Diver lets the girls in his houses get high."

"What if you don't have insurance?"

"Then they don't give a fuck about you."

"How many bedrooms per house?" asked Mac.

"Four bedrooms. Two girls per room."

"So that's eight girls per house. What's rent?"

"I pay $850 a week."

"Eight-fifty a week for each girl? That's $6,800 a week," Mac said.

"Per house."

Mac switched his phone to the calculator. "That's over $27,000 a month per house. The Deaver brothers own six sober homes. That's over $160,000 a month."

"Crazy money," Sadie said. "And that doesn't count the drug tests."

"That's almost two million dollars a year in rent."

Roxanne looked at Mac. "Looks like you've got your story."

Sadie asked, "What story?"

"Don't worry about it," Mac said. "But you've been a big help."

Sadie's demeanor changed. She had that look of someone who just figured out they'd been speaking without thinking. "I appreciate the coffee and all," she said, "but seriously, who the fuck are you guys? Am I in trouble?"

"No, honey, you're not in any trouble at all," Roxanne said.

"Is Maggie in trouble? She'd probably kill me if I told you she was dating Diver. She has a boyfriend back home."

"Maggie's not in trouble either."

"Can you drive me back to Crossroad's Club? There's another meeting at nine, and my shit is court-ordered."

"We'll drive you back," Mac said.

*****

"What a fucking racket," Roxanne said as she and Mac drove back up to the hotel. "The cops are in on it all. They're in on it!"

Mac pulled back into the Marriott and tossed the keys to Bobby.

Roxanne continued, "This can't be legal."

"You think Hanrahan could check the legality of it? Or at least have someone at the *Post* look into it? I doubt the research department in Aspen would be useful for this."

"Probably not until tomorrow. I'm sure he's passed out by now. He's a day drinker."

"The homes are technically owned by an LLC, but it's not hard to trace the LLC back to the Deaver brothers," Mac said. "All this information is online."

Mac and Roxanne strolled through the lobby and entered the elevator. They walked down the carpeted hallway and entered Mac's hotel room. Roxanne flopped on the bed with her arms outstretched. Mac grabbed a Heineken from the minifridge and popped the top.

"I've been prowling NA meetings for two months looking for information you dug up in three days," she lamented.

"What can I say? I'm a professional."

"But I thought you covered live music and wrote about local bands."

"Funny."

"Seriously. I think your editor is going to freak out. What's his name—Charlie? You nailed this story."

Mac took a sip of his beer. "Yeah, I've been thinking about that," he said. "You think Hanrahan would want this story instead? Don't you think it hits harder if it runs in the *Palm Beach Post*? Seems like local news should get a crack at it."

"Personally, I've never really understood the Aspen angle."

"I'm serious. What if I pitch this story to Hanrahan instead? We can combine sources."

Roxanne rolled onto her belly and kicked her heels toward the back of her head. She looked like a scorpion. "What about your boss?"

"What if I don't go back to Aspen?"

"At all?"

"You heard what Hanrahan said, one of his reporters just took a job at the *Washington Post*. It sounds like there's an opening here."

"And just like that, you'd quit your job and move here? I don't think you'll get to keep the hotel suite and Mustang."

Mac walked across the room and opened the curtains and French doors. He looked out at the Atlantic Ocean and took in a deep breath. "I'm getting sick of Aspen. I like it here," he said.

Roxanne rolled around in the bed some more. "Are you hungry?" she asked.

"Starving. What are you in the mood for?"

"What were you thinking?"

"Anywhere. Pick a place. Compliments of the *Aspen Daily News*."

"Let's just order room service, a bottle of nice champagne, and fuck all night."

Mac said, "Sure."

FRIDAY

Roxanne woke up early and was in the bathroom when the pounding on the door started. It definitely wasn't housekeeping, Mac thought, climbing out of bed. The pounding continued. Mac wrapped a Marriott towel around his waist and stuck his eye to the peephole. It was two Delray Beach police officers. One of them punched the peephole. The other kicked the bottom of the door.

"Open up, McCaffrey!"

Mac opened the bathroom door. Roxanne was standing frozen, naked, with a toothbrush in her mouth.

"Lock the door and don't come out," he said. "No matter what." He closed the door.

Mac put on his white Marriott robe and snatched some items from the desk, stuffing them in his pockets. The pounding continued.

"We can hear you shuffling around in there. Open the fucking door."

Mac opened the door a crack. "Good morning," he said.

Officer Morris kicked the door in and immediately forced himself into the room. Mac backed up.

Detective Deaver followed into the room and closed the door behind him.

"Oh, look, it's Crockett and Tubbs," Mac said.

"Have a seat," Deaver said.

"I'd rather stand."

Morris gut-punched Mac and shoved him on the bed. He put his forearm across his head and shoved a knee into his back.

"Oh, I like it rough, you big stud," Mac said.

"Get off him."

Morris stood up and gave Mac a shove. He rolled over and sat on the edge of the bed. "You could have bought me dinner first, honey."

"Fuck you, dickhead," Morris said.

"I don't suppose you have a warrant?" Mac asked.

"We don't need one. You let us in."

Mac looked at Detective Deaver. "What do you want? I thought our date was on Tuesday."

"Change of plans," he said. "Did you really think you could trust a junkie?"

"What junkie?"

"If you think for one shimmering moment I'm going to let you fuck with my real-estate investments, you're dumber than those ugly-ass Hawaiian shirts you wear."

"Real-estate investments? Is that what you're calling it?"

"Yes. My brother and I own real estate in this town. We own rental properties, and there's nothing more to it."

"You own corrupt sober living homes, and you know it. So do I. It's an insurance scam to boot."

"I provide young wayward youth with a safe place to stay while they achieve sobriety."

"You blackmail them into renting from you."

Morris gave Mac a backhand and shoved him down on the bed. Mac bounced back up into a seated position.

Deaver continued, "If you don't back the fuck off this story and leave my tenants alone, we're going to pursue a murder investigation against you."

"Murder? Are we playing *Clue*? Did I murder Miss Scarlet in the library with the candlestick?"

"Leonard 'Leaky' Lapahie was last seen in your company where several witnesses saw you consume an excessive amount of booze with a known alcoholic. The two of you left the bar together, and Leaky mysteriously ends up hit by a train. Maybe the evidence suggests he was pushed."

"You've been watching too much *Forensic Files*, Serpico."

"Are you really challenging me to build my case?"

"The evidence shows that we didn't leave the bar together. There's CCTV video from the bar. You said so yourself."

"Yeah, about that…According to the bartender that night, there was a malfunction with the security cams. There's no footage of either one of you leaving."

"*Anymore*, you mean. There's no footage anymore."

"We got a witness saying you two were arguing over a game of darts. You were mad about a three-hundred-dollar bar tab he didn't help pay. The two of you were observed fighting and arguing when you stumbled out extremely intoxicated."

"That's bullshit. The bartender told me I left before Leaky. There was no argument, and that bar tab was paid by the *Aspen Daily News*. It wasn't even my money."

"Do you really think O'Connor's is willing to put its liquor license on the line for you? Overserving a known alcoholic is frowned upon by the Division of Alcoholic Beverages and Tobacco. They're going to say what I want them to say, or I'll have that shithole shuttered for good. The city would probably give me an award for closing that dive."

"With absolutely no respect at all, you have no case. If you did have enough evidence, you'd take me in now."

"I'm giving you a chance, McCaffrey."

"You're canning my story."

"Homicide thinks we have a good enough case to lock you up until an arraignment. Do you wanna lay around the beach for the next few days sipping cocktails or get locked up in county jail where *cock* and *tail* take on a whole new meaning?"

"What do you want?"

"I want you to stop investigating my real-estate investments and kill your pathetic little newspaper story. Go back to your mountain town and pretend like you've never heard of Delray Beach."

"And if I don't, you're going to falsify murder charges against me? I'm pretty sure that's extortion, and in most states, even Florida, extortion is a crime."

"Not as punishable as a murder charge."

"I don't know how happy my editor is going to be if I don't have a story to print. That's kind of an important element when it comes to publishing a newspaper. You know, printing articles. It's a key factor in the newspaper model."

"That's not my problem. But whatever you write, if you mention my name or my brother's name, I will have you extradited back to Florida, and I will charge you with murdering Leonard Lapahie. And that's after I have Morris here stick a soldering iron up your ass."

"Plugged in?"

Morris smacked Mac again.

"Fine. There's no story," Mac said. "I'll tell my editor there's nothing here. And I'll go back to Aspen."

"That's probably the smartest decision you've made all week," Deaver said. "Don't fuck with me, paper boy."

Deaver and Morris walked out of the hotel room and slammed the door behind them. Mac stood up and rubbed his ribs.

"Are you okay?" he asked. "You can come out."

Roxanne rushed out of the bathroom and came to Mac. Unfortunately, she was no longer naked.

"I'm fine. What about you?"

"Why'd you get dressed?"

"Who were those guys?" Roxanne asked.

"Oh, them? Those guys are fascists."

"That was Deaver's brother?"

"Yeah. I guess one of the girls shot her mouth off. Apparently, a nine-dollar cup of coffee wasn't enough to keep Sadie's mouth shut."

"What are you going to do?"

"Just because I can't investigate the story anymore doesn't mean we can't give it to someone else. Come on, let's get Hanrahan involved. This story is better for the *Post* anyway."

Mac rubbed his rib cage some more. It didn't feel cracked, but Morris packed a punch.

"What about your editor in Aspen?"

"I'll explain the situation to him."

"Do you think he'll believe you?"

Mac reached into the pocket of his hotel robe and pulled out a slim black Sony recording device. "It's all on record," he said. "This is a digital voice recorder."

Roxanne smiled. "Oh, you're my hero, Bernie Mac."

"I use this to record the bands I cover back home. It's a handy device. I never thought I'd use it during a shakedown."

"Now what?"

"I think I should probably check out of this hotel for starters."

"You can stay with me."

"I was thinking about ditching town for a few days. I should probably get away from Delray Beach and lay low. You wanna come with me?"

"Where were you thinking?"

"Do you have any recommendations?"

"Yeah, I know the perfect spot to disappear for a while."

"Is it close?"

"It's close to Cuba…"

*****

Key West, Florida, is the southernmost point in the continental United States. Mac hadn't known this until he saw it etched into the concrete-anchored buoy at the intersection of Whitehead and South Street. Tourists lined up to take pictures. Golf carts and mopeds whizzed by. Mac and Roxanne held hands as they walked past the marker.

"We're only ninety miles to Cuba from here?" Mac asked.

"Yeah, long way from Aspen."

"Do you come here a lot?"

"When I want to get away, sure. There's nothing like Key West. I like it there."

Mac and Roxanne stopped at a café and ordered café con leche. Several colorful roosters ambled around the street.

Mac asked, "What's with the roosters?"

"They're symbiotic with Key West. Colorful and loud. Just like the people."

"How'd they get here?"

"Cockfighting. It was popular in Cuba, and it came here along with them. It was outlawed in the seventies, and the roosters took over. Personally, I think they've earned the right to stay."

Mac sipped his coffee and continued people-watching. Somebody walked by carrying two enormous macaws. Another guy sat on a street corner weaving hats out of green palm fronds. Mac pulled his phone out and noticed a few missed calls from the *Aspen Daily News*.

"Shit," he said. "It's the paper. I missed three calls."

"You should probably call them."

"Do you mind?"

"Of course not."

Mac got up, stepped off the porch of the café, and took a short walk. He hit the call button on his phone.

"Mac," said a panicked voice.

"Yeah, Charlie."

"Where are you? Why did you check out of the Marriott?"

"How did you know I checked out?"

"I've been trying to reach you. The concierge said you checked out. Peril is going insane about the bill. Your expenses, Mac."

Mac quickly changed the subject. "The cops are pissed, Charlie. I think I stepped in shit."

"Where are you?" Charlie asked.

Mac watched the sailboats float by off the Southernmost Point. Pelicans flew in formation overhead.

"I don't think I wanna tell you that right now, Charlie."

"You wanna tell me who you're with?"

"I don't think I'll tell you that, either."

"I have a pretty good guess."

"I'm sure you do."

"Peril is livid. You might get yourself fired this time."

"What's his problem?"

"He was in a budget meeting with the publishers all morning. Your expenses, Mac—what the fuck are you thinking?"

"I have receipts."

"I'm telling you, Peril is fuming."

"Fuck him, Charlie. This whole thing was his idea. I didn't think this was going to work out in the first place. I didn't think there was a story here. I said that from the jump. There's no Aspen angle. Nobody cares about Conrad Harvey, except maybe his daughter."

"And *that* was the story you were supposed to be working on. Roxanne Harvey was the story, remember?"

"She's not a drunk. I'm not going to slander her," Mac said. "What about Stransky? I still don't know why she's being followed."

Mac could hear screaming from the newsroom. It was coming closer, and it sounded like a familiar nasal-voiced asshole he knew well.

"Is that McCaffrey on the line?"

Mac could hear the phone getting ripped from Charlie's hands. It didn't sound like he put up much of a struggle.

"Have you lost your fucking mind, Bernard?"

"Oh, hey, Chief. Please, call me Mac."

"You're done. The credit card is canceled. You mind telling me how...or why...you decided to upgrade your hotel room to a $500-per-night suite?"

"The ocean view."

"And the convertible?"

"I look good in red."

"And $375 at...O'Connor's? What's O'Connor's?"

"Drinks with a source. I have a receipt."

"You're buying drinks at The Breakers on Palm Beach island? The tiki bar at the Marriott, The Dune Deck...Boston's on the Beach...Two Georges... Look at this bill..."

"I have receipts."

"What do you expect me to tell the publisher, smart-ass?" said Peril. "You got no story and racked up expenses that more than double your paycheck. You haven't even been gone a week."

"Tell them whatever you want. They have the budget for it."

"How do you know what the budget is? You're a fucking local music critic, Bernard. You don't know shit. And now you're done. You're done. Do you understand me?"

"Whatever you say, Chief."

"I'm having your desk packed up this afternoon. We'll mail your personal items to your shitty little apartment. I never want to see you in this newsroom again."

Mac chose his next words carefully. "Did you break the news to Amy in the photo department?" he asked.

There was a pause on the other end of the line.

"What did you say?"

"You heard me."

"Why would it matter to Amy in the photo department?"

"I don't think she's going back to beef jerky after she's tried the filet, Chief."

There was another pause.

"Listen to me, you little shit. Whatever you think you know, you don't know."

"Whatever I know, I don't know? Did you guys order Chinese food for lunch today? Because it sounds like you're reading me a fortune cookie."

"You're fired! How's that for a fortune?"

"If you fire me, I'm gonna tell your wife you've been sleeping with a girl in the photo department that's the same age as your daughter. So you can go fuck yourself, Chief. You're a hack journalist anyway. You don't deserve the staff you have. Even Patrick Hanrahan at the *Palm Beach Post* thinks you're a piece of shit. And he's right."

"Pat Hanrahan? Pat Hanrahan? Yeah, well, I just spoke to that princess the other day, and he says you're…"

Peril was still screaming when Mac hung up the phone. He walked back to Ana's Cuban Café where Roxanne was still sipping her coffee and looking beautiful.

"How'd that go?"

"Great. I might get a raise," Mac said.

"Did you tell them about the cops?"

"Kinda."

"Kinda?"

"I started to, and then the conversation sorta changed. It's fine," Mac said.

Mac took a seat across from Roxanne. She was wearing her floppy white sun hat and big black sunglasses that made her features look small. Mac smiled at her. He could tell she had just applied lipstick. It was pink.

"I don't think I want to go back to Aspen," he said. "I think it's time we call Hanrahan and give the story to the *Post*. I can't take a byline on this story, of course. But I can point Pat in the right direction, and I can be his source. All the property records are online. I have the story. It's pretty tight. I think he can probably get it in the Sunday paper."

"What about the Aspen paper? Won't you get in trouble if you don't write the story for the newspaper that sent you here? What did they just say to you? What did you say to them?"

"Talk to Pat. If there's room at the *Palm Beach Post* for me, I have no use for the *Aspen Daily News* anymore. I think I'd rather be in Florida. The Aspen paper has lost interest in the story, and I think I'm losing interest in them."

"I think I'd rather you be in Florida too, Mac, but I don't think you should quit your job and move across the country on a whim. Is there something you're leaving out? Is there something you're not telling me?"

Mac avoided the question.

"Hanrahan could run this story with just the property records. Those records alone, when cross-referenced with the sober house registrations, prove a cop with Delray PD owns six zoned half-way houses. Then we have the story Maggie told us and the audio recording of Deaver talking about his real-estate investments. We have it."

"Can we finally talk about the elephant in the room?"

"We're outside, and those are roosters. I don't see any elephants."

"Who is Leaky, and why are the cops saying you murdered him?"

"Oh, that."

"I didn't think I'd have to ask why the cops came to your hotel this morning, but clearly you're not going to tell me."

"Leaky was my original source on this story," Mac said. "We got drunk on Tuesday night, and he fell in front of a train after he left the bar."

"Holy shit, Mac. Did you see this happen? He fell in front of a train? Is he dead?"

"Death is usually the result of getting hit by a train, yes."

"Were you there?"

"I wasn't around for the accident."

"I'm not suggesting you pushed him."

"I wasn't driving the train either."

"Mac, this is serious."

"The cops know it was an accident. The bartender originally said I left before the guy, and Deaver said he saw surveillance video from the bar that showed me walking out first."

"It was hard to hear through the bathroom door. But it sounded like there's no more surveillance video," Roxanne said.

"I think they destroyed it."

"If Hanrahan runs your story, don't you think the cops will figure out you're the source?"

"Maybe. But I'm not going to let it stop me. I didn't get into journalism to kowtow to people in power. Especially not cops. In fact, my ambitions have always been the opposite of that."

"You're cute up there on that soapbox."

Mac's phone rung again. This time, it was Charlie's cell phone.

"I have to take this again. I'm sorry," Mac said. "Give Hanrahan a call and see what he says."

Mac stepped off the café porch and answered the call. He could tell Charlie was smoking a cigarette. He was probably outside in the *News* parking lot.

"Am I really fired?" Mac asked.

"I dunno, kid. Something is going on with the publishers. They were kinda pissed about the expenses earlier, but Peril somehow smoothed that over. He's definitely got you for insubordination though."

"Insubordination? In high school, that barely qualified me for detention."

"That's part of the problem, Mac. You're still treating this job like it's fucking high school. You're out there on a pussy hunt and getting drunk with your sources. For Christ's sake, even when you're here, you're trying to fuck every female on staff."

"Not the fat ones."

"You've been there less than a week. You maxed your expense account, your source is fucking dead, the cops are somehow involved. You've got no story. You haven't even filed any copy."

"I've got a hell of a story, Charlie."

"What story, Mac? It's not the story Peril wanted."

"First, he wanted me to write about Conrad Harvey's kid being an alcoholic and that story was debunked. Then he wanted me to find out why she's being followed, and less than a day later, he spiked that story too. What is he so pissed about?"

"Your expenses, dipshit, for starters. Not only was this a wasted trip, you jacked up that expense account in a big way."

Mac said, "Fuck him."

"Did you find out why the Harvey broad has a private investigator following her?"

"Not yet. I'm still sorta working on that. Does Peril still want that story?"

"Did you hear him? No fucking way, kid."

"What am I supposed to do?"

"Technically, he can't fire you over the phone, at least that's what human resources said. At the very least, he can't fire you while you're on assignment. I think he also needs the publishers to check off on it. Maybe that's what they're talking about."

"He said he canceled the credit card. How am I supposed to get back?"

"The return flight is open-ended. You can fly back whenever you want. The hotel and per diem is gone. You're on your own for food and shelter."

"What about the car?"

"I can't tell you how to handle that, but I would just drop it off and get on a plane. Maybe you should fly back pronto and try and salvage your job. I have a hard time believing you have any money saved up. I know what you get paid, kid. None of us got into this business for the paycheck. How long do you really think you'll last in Florida with limited funds and no expense account?"

Mac crunched some financials in his head. It didn't take him long. "I think the cops still want my statement on Tuesday regarding the Leaky matter."

"You could leave anyway. You never got a subpoena."

"I think I'm gonna stick around until at least Tuesday," Mac said.

"What are you gonna do until then?"

"I've considered nude modeling."

"Maybe you'd be better at that."

"Maybe."

"If you need money, let me know. I can help you out short-term if you need it."

"Thanks, Dad, but please don't tell Mom."

"I'm serious. Just let me know. I'll try and calm down Peril and keep him away from your desk."

"Hey, Charlie?"

"Yeah, kid."

Charlie sounded beaten down, like he, too, was growing tired of Mac's self-sabotaging ways.

"Do you remember that time Peril's office smelled like a sushi restaurant dumpster for two weeks?"

"Yeah, how could I forget? I had to sit through the editorial meetings with everyone gagging and holding their breath."

"I did that."

"Did what?"

"I took a can of tuna fish and stabbed holes in it with a screwdriver. Then I taped it under his desk. I didn't know it would take him two weeks to find it."

"What the fuck is this, confession?"

"No, I just never got to tell anyone."

"Well, thanks for sharing, I guess, you fucking weirdo. Why did you do that? His office had to be sterilized after that."

"Peril is a bully. But he's also a coward. I just wanted to anonymously prank him and let him know he can still be fucked with."

"So you stunk up his office? Mac, that's really weird."

"He's never liked me, Charlie."

"You walk around the office barefoot, you fucked his mistress, and you made his office smell like rotten pussy for a month."

"I still think he sent me out here on a setup. This story was a setup."

"He's not the one that jacked up the expenses, kid. That was all you."

"Why are we in this business if not for the expense account?"

"What happened to your speech about journalistic integrity?"

"I can have integrity while driving a Mustang convertible. These things aren't mutually exclusive."

"Maybe not," Charlie said.

Mac stood on the corner of Simonton Street in Key West. He looked down at his flip-flops and said nothing.

"Look," Charlie said. "Take care of yourself out there and call me if you need money."

Mac said thank you and hung up the phone. He walked back to Roxanne just as she was ending her call with Hanrahan.

"You're my favorite, Pat," she said. "I'll tell him right now."

She hung up the phone and smiled at Mac.

"Good news," she said. "Pat is all in on the story. He's got a beat reporter that covers real estate that's fact-checking the property records now. He said Sunday is a push, but it can definitely run Monday. He said he can go page 1."

"Is he going to seek comment from the police chief or the PIO?"

"What's PIO?"

"That's the Public Information Officer. They usually handle the press. Someone is going to have to call the cops for comment."

"I have no idea. Pat said he's going to have the property records checked out and he's going to go himself to door-knock the halfway houses and see if he can get any of the girls on the record."

"Did you tell him about Sadie?"

"Yes."

"Did you tell him about my lover's quarrel with Delray PD?"

"Yeah, he called them a bunch of pussycats."

"That's what he said?"

"Yeah. He said the Delray Police Department is filled with a bunch of pussycats. That's verbatim, what he said."

"So now what?"

"What do you mean?"

"What are we gonna do in Key West while Hanrahan works the story?"

"Remember when I told you I was in a punk band when I was a kid?"

"How could I forget Bashful Anus?"

"The bass player is still a friend of mine. We've known each other for almost twenty years. He's a bartender at the Green Parrot. I figure we can crash at his place. He's got a duplex on the island, and he rents half of it out. If it's vacant, he'll let us stay there."

"What time do they open?"

"The Green Parrot? The bars are always open in Key West. We'll make it there eventually."

*****

Even though Key West is only two hundred miles south of Palm Beach, the weather seemed noticeably warmer. Roxanne and Mac strolled along the water past the Hemingway House and the Key West Lighthouse, turning down Duval Street and walking all the way to Mallory Square at the west end of the island.

"This is the best place on the island to watch the sunset," Roxanne said, clasping Mac's hand in hers.

"I could get used to it," Mac said. "I don't like Aspen this time of year. Spring is wet. The ski season is over, and there's a lull before the summer tourists."

"Where are you from, Mac? You mentioned living in Denver. I just assumed you're from there. But were you born in Colorado?"

"I'm actually from upstate New York. I grew up outside of Albany," Mac said.

"When did you move to Colorado?"

"Right after high school. I didn't even look at colleges back east. I applied to almost every school in Colorado. Boulder was a little too pretentious so I went to Colorado State."

"Fort Collins?"

"Yup. Go Rams."

"You think Boulder is pretentious, and you live in Aspen?"

"Touché."

"I told you we still have property in Aspen."

"I have a feeling your accommodations are mildly superior to mine."

"It's a big ranch like the one we have in Wellington," said Roxanne. "And we have a condo in Snowmass Village."

"I have a studio apartment," Mac said. "It's a piece of shit, but I can walk to work. Can I ask you a question now?"

"I would expect nothing less from a reporter."

"I meet rich women all the time in Aspen. The ones that take a shine to me are usually just slumming it with a townie. You're nothing like those women, but I need to ask why somebody of your caliber is interested in hanging around with me?"

"My caliber? Your insecurity is charming, if not a little out of character."

"We're definitely from different worlds. Economically speaking, obviously."

"What can I say? I like your stupid shirts, and I find journalists sexy."

Mac looked at his shirt. It was the blue one with the palm trees.

"I know a lot of journalists," he said, "and I wouldn't call many of us sexy. My friend Charlie back in Aspen looks like Dr. Evil and smells like cigarettes and gin."

"Sounds a lot like Pat Hanrahan."

"I met Pat. He's a better dresser," Mac said.

Roxanne and Mac stopped to watch the booze-cruise catamarans head out to sea carrying groups of boisterous tourists. Reggae music echoed across the water.

"What about music? I told you I like punk rock. What do you listen to?" Roxanne asked.

"We doing small talk?" Mac asked.

"You've seen my vagina. I think it's fair that you tell me what kind of music you like."

"I like everything except country. I really like eighties Britpop. Joy Division, New Order. I'm really still into the nineties grunge scene. That was real to me."

"That explains your ripped jeans."

"That's not a grunge thing. That's just my refusal to try and purchase jeans in Aspen on my budget. We don't exactly have a Target there."

"So Nirvana or Pearl Jam?"

"Pearl Jam."

"Who's a better singer, Kurt or Eddie?"

"Chris Cornell."

"Does the band have to come from Seattle to really be considered grunge?"

"That's a good question. A lot of bands from the era weren't from Seattle, but I do think the

Washington bands had a more distinct sound. Heavy power chords, simple time signatures…I dunno how to explain it. Maybe they all used the same amps."

"Do you play any instruments?"

"I'm tone deaf and have no rhythm. What about you? How come you didn't stick with Bashful Anus?"

Roxanne laughed and shook her head. "We were kids. We played in my dad's barn. Half the band could hardly play their instruments."

"That didn't stop the Sex Pistols."

"No, I guess it didn't. We were in middle school. It was just for kicks."

"After that, I mean. If you wanted to be a singer, I'm sure your father could have paid for studio time. You probably had some advantages there. Coulda gone to art school. You definitely have the look for it."

"I think my father assumed it was just a phase after my mom died. Once I got older and we moved to the ranch in Wellington, I spent more time with the horses. Most of my friends from back then went away to college, and we lost touch. My dad didn't want me seeking fame. There was a lot of media coverage after Mom died. My dad didn't want that for me."

Mac ordered a couple of margaritas from a kiosk bar. They kept walking along the water.

"Have you ever been married?" Mac asked.

"God, no. Dating in my twenties was basically a who's who of Palm Beach socialite offspring trying to get into my pants. I would go out with these guys a couple of times, and they all annoyed me. I'm not impressed with wealth or power. The typical rich asshole in Palm Beach thinks money turns everyone on. I don't really need any more money, so why would I be impressed with somebody else's fortune?"

"I guess you wouldn't be."

"Donald Trump Jr. was trying to go out with me when I was still a teenager. It was creepy."

"Trump Jr. is a douchebag. He used to bartend in Aspen. He was a fucking drunk back then. Nobody in town liked him. Even with all that money, he had no friends."

"Imagine cloning fifty more of him. That's what dating was like in Palm Beach in my twenties."

"I can understand now why you're single."

"What about you?" Roxanne asked. "Have you ever been married?"

"I was close once. My college girlfriend and I moved in with each other. She came to Aspen with me but left after a year. She moved back to Kansas City. That's where she was from."

"What did she do?"

"She worked at one of the hotels as a concierge. Hospitality wasn't really her beat. She studied philosophy in school. I'm not sure what she expected to do with that degree anyway. We talked about Nietzsche a lot," Mac said. "Well, *she* talked about Nietzsche a lot."

"Why did you guys break up?"

"You mean besides the exhilarating talks about German existentialism? I worked nights for the most part, she worked days. I was drinking with the bands all night. I think I unintentionally ignored her. Journalists don't make the best romantic partners."

Roxanne asked, "Why do you say that?"

"We're all narcissists. We all want to see our name in print. It's ego."

"Is that right?"

"We know everything. We drink a lot."

"Are you reading me your Tinder profile?"

"No, I'm just saying…I've been around a lot of these guys. Most of the guys I know are divorced and spend more time being married to the newspaper."

"But you like it?"

"I love being in a newsroom. I'm sad the industry is gasping its last breath. Nobody reads the newspaper anymore. It's all online or television."

"So why do you stick with it?"

"I like getting ink on my fingers."

"Well, I think you're a good journalist, Mac," said Roxanne. "Even if you did murder one of your sources."

"You're hilarious."

"Pat sounded excited about the leads you dug up. He's not an easy guy to impress."

"Let's wait and see how hard the story hits."

"Are you nervous about the cops looking for you after the story runs?"

"They're not likely to find me in Key West."

"I mean, when we get back."

"Fuck those guys. Small-town cops don't really scare me. They're pussycats, remember? Isn't that what Hanrahan said?"

"You're so brave, Bernard McCaffrey."

"Of course, I am. I told you about my Medal of Honor when we met."

"Be honest, has that line ever worked?"

"Excluding present company? No. Never."

"I'm not sure what that says about me."

"I wouldn't seek therapy over it."

"I guess I like a guy with a confident line of bullshit and some charm."

"Are you calling me charming?" asked Mac.

"I guess I am."

"I've been called worse."

"I know. A few hours ago, a cop called you a dickhead."

"I've been called worse than that too."

They continued walking, passing by street vendors and some busking musicians. Mac watched one of them playing Hendrix on a banjo. He tossed a few singles into the open guitar case, which was being suspiciously guarded by a gray house cat.

"It really wasn't the bullshit line you gave me, you know," Roxanne said. "Or the charm."

"My striking good looks?"

"You seemed passionate about the story you're writing. That got me thinking about Juliette. It was curious running into someone so randomly that was looking for some of the same information I was.

Especially somebody from Aspen. What are the chances?"

"I'm pretty sure if you threw a rock in Delray Beach, you'd hit somebody that's been affected by the rehab scene."

"I guess that's true. But you don't find it coincidental?"

"You were sitting by yourself, and you're the most beautiful woman I've ever seen in my life. I would have never been able to live with myself if I didn't at least say hello."

"I guess you're missing my point."

Mac stopped walking and faced Roxanne. He looked her in her eyes and put his hand on her wrist.

"Do I believe in fate? Sure," he said. "Coincidence? Maybe. Do I look at you and I here, right now, in Key West...and think I'm dreaming? Unquestionably."

"Do you want me to pinch you?"

Mac said, "Absolutely not."

*****

After the sunset and an irresponsible amount of tequila, Roxanne and Mac finally found their way to the Green Parrot, a local dive music venue on Whitehead Street, where Roxanne's friend was working as a bartender. The place had a local vibe, Mac thought, as he straddled a wooden barstool and tried to act sober.

Roxanne meandered her way down to the service bar and surprised the bartender, who looked up at her with elation. He resembled a young Jerry Garcia, with a thick bushy beard, potbelly, and wire-rimmed glasses.

"Roxanne Harvey!" he said, giving her a boisterous bear hug.

"Hey, Chipmunk."

"What are you doing here? How long are you staying?"

"Not long. Can we crash with you?"

"Absolutely," he said. "New renters won't be down until next week. The place is all yours. It's so good to see you."

Roxanne said, "Likewise."

She motioned for Mac to join her. He slipped off his barstool and walked toward them.

Mac stuck out his hand. "Chipmunk, is it?"

"It's Alvin. She's been calling me Chipmunk since we were kids."

"It's nice to meet you," Mac said.

"Let me get you some drinks. Usual for you, Roxy?"

"Of course."

"Mac, what's your potion?"

"Heineken is good."

Chipmunk reached into an icebox and pulled out a Heineken, popping the top off on a brass mermaid screwed to the wall behind him, and then went to work on Roxanne's always-confusing margarita order.

"Decent band tonight," he said. "They're in town from Saint Pete. Mostly covers, but they sound great."

"Mac covers live music for the *Aspen Daily News*," Roxanne said.

"Right on. Aspen, huh? You're a long way from home."

"I get the impression Key West is a long way from home for a lot of people."

"It's either a long way from home, or it *is* home, brother."

Chipmunk slid Roxanne's drink down in front of her and poured himself a shot of rum from the well.

"Here's to alcohol and contraceptives," he said. "Cheers."

All three clinked glasses. The band was warming up, and Mac turned and watched them tuning the guitars and hooking up the amps. The drummer was screwing on the toms. Somebody was tinkering with the mixer.

Chipmunk leaned in closer to Roxanne and touched her hand. "I heard about your father," he said. "Saw it on the news. I'm sorry for your loss, honey."

"I assumed you saw it. It's still on TV."

"I just really wanted to offer heartfelt condolences," Chipmunk said.

"Thank you. He was old. It's okay. It really is. Let's just have a good time."

Mac listened to the band tuning their instruments. He had a confident buzz. "*Hey*!" he yelled to the band. "You guys know any Blondie?"

"No, no, no," Roxanne said nervously.

"Oh, shit," added Chipmunk, "my man *does* know you. Here we go."

"I'm not singing," Roxanne said unconvincingly.

"I got a girl here who wants to sing 'Call Me.' Do you guys know that one? She used to be in Bashful Anus. You ever heard of them?"

The guitar player played a few licks and looked at the rest of the band, who all seemed to nod in agreement. He turned back around toward the bar.

"Yeah, we can do it," he said. "The Blondie tune. Not sure about the anal stuff. You wanna kick off the set?"

Roxanne looked at Mac. "You really want to see this?" she asked.

"Of course he does," Chipmunk said.

"Go show me how punk rock Blondie really is," Mac said.

By now, the crowd was hip to the surroundings, and some yips of encouragement rang out. Roxanne took a big-girl sip of her margarita, tossed her hat on the bar, and shook out her blond pixie locks. She kissed Mac on the mouth. The crowd started clapping.

She said, "I'll be right back."

"Oh, I'm not going anywhere," Mac said, leaning back on the bar.

Roxanne worked her way to the stage, slinking her long legs past the enthusiastic mix of tourists and locals.

"You're gonna like this," Chipmunk said, putting his fingers in his mouth and letting loose an ear-piercing whistle.

"We're gonna get a little help kicking things off tonight," one of the band members said into the mic. "Why don't you tell us who you are?"

Roxanne bounded on stage. She took a slight bow, and the crowd was immediately hers.

"My name is Roxanne," she said.

The crowd roared with approval.

Roxanne huddled with the band for a moment, and they bantered back and forth. The singer passed her the microphone.

"Thanks for letting me do this, everyone. This is one of my favorites," she said into the mic. "We're taking this back to 1980…This is 'Call Me' by Blondie."

The familiar chords began to thump. Roxanne started shimmying. The crowd stood up as the lyrics came in…

"*Color me your color, baby, color me your car… Color me your color, darling, I know who you are…*"

The band didn't miss a beat, playing as if it was a set staple. Roxanne continued to hit the notes.

"*Call me…on the line, call me, call me anytime… Call me, you can call me any day or night…Call me.*"

After the bridge, the crowd was wild. Roxanne stalked the stage like a lioness. She ripped into the second verse, staring across the bar at Mac.

"Cover me with kisses, baby, cover me with love… Roll me in designer sheets, I'll never get enough… Emotions come, I don't know why, cover up love's alibi…"

The crowd was hanging on every word, entranced by Roxanne's effortless charisma. She slapped a few high fives, preparing for the chorus and finale. She shook her head back and forth, leaned back, and let it rip.

"Call me!…on the line…Call me any day or night…Call me… And I'll arrive anytime…Call me!"

Roxanne flipped the mic back to the lead singer, stretched her arms over her head, and let out one final, sexy shimmy and drew raucous applause.

Chipmunk leaned over the bar behind Mac. "Debbie Harry is rolling in her grave," he said.

Mac looked over his shoulder. "Debbie Harry isn't dead."

Chipmunk said, "Whatever, man."

For a rare, fleeting moment, Mac was speechless. Roxanne accepted her ovation and came bounding back over to the bar as the band ripped into a Ramones song, not missing a beat. She was sexy and sweaty. She collapsed into Mac's lap.

"Was that punk rock enough for you, motherfucker?" she said.

SATURDAY

CHIPMUNK'S DUPLEX WAS IN THE Historic District of Key West, not far from the cemetery and located on Pine Street. The walk home from Green Parrot had been a bit of a stumble, but the king-sized bed they collapsed into was cozy.

Mac awoke with Roxanne's naked body draped across his as the sun came up. A sliver of sunshine snuck through the curtains, leaving a perfect sliver of light blazing across the bed.

He was only slightly awake when Chipmunk cracked the door and peeked in, wearing a diving mask and snorkel. He threw a pair of board shorts at Mac, which landed squarely on his face.

"Put those on," Chipmunk said. "We're going to get breakfast."

"What time is it?"

"Time to get breakfast, dummy."

Mac looked at Chipmunk's getup. "What the fuck are you wearing?" he asked.

"We're going to get breakfast."

"Are you searching for Atlantis?"

Chipmunk wasn't amused. "Let's go. Come on," he said.

Mac looked at the blond mop of hair stuffed into his armpit. "Should I wake her up?"

"You just did," said a muffled voice.

"No, you sleep in. We'll be back," Chipmunk said.

"Coffee and mimosas," Roxanne said. "I don't care in what order."

Mac slipped out of bed and into the shorts. Chipmunk tossed a second mask and snorkel at him. "Let's go get us some lobsters."

"*Coffee and mimosas*," came a louder request. "And bacon."

"Table will be set in an hour, Roxy," Chipmunk said. "Let's go, dude."

Mac and Chipmunk stepped off his porch and walked to a lime-green golf cart parked on the pebble driveway. Mac slapped sunglasses on his face.

"Nice whip," he said. "Was this here last night?"

"Yeah."

"I did not notice."

Mac and Chipmunk hopped into the golf cart and headed off toward the gulf.

Mac fumbled with the mask and snorkel in his hands. He turned around and saw a couple of sets of diving flippers, two fishing nets, and what looked like a fetish whip stuffed into the basket attached to the golf cart.

"What the fuck is this? Are we playing with kittens?" Mac asked, grabbing the flimsy rod.

"It's a tickle stick. It's for lobstering."

"You must know some kinky lobsters."

Mac flicked the stick around like he was taunting a cat.

"Lobsters crawl under the rocks and into the reef backward. We're gonna poke 'em with that thing and scoot 'em into the net."

"We? I'm diving for lobsters?"

"Yeah, don't be a pussy. It's only four feet of water. Once we grab three or four, we're out of there."

Mac flicked at Chipmunk with the tickle stick.

"Stop it, shit head," he said. "Quit playing around."

Chipmunk rolled the golf cart down a rocky path and to a small parking lot adjacent to a small inlet. Mac noticed a few bodies floating in the water about twenty yards offshore.

"Grab some fins and a net," Chipmunk said.

Mac did as ordered, and the two walked to the rocky shore. Mac dipped his toes in the water. It was much warmer than he had expected.

Chipmunk pulled off his tattered Sublime T-shirt, revealing a full body of hair and a noteworthy beer gut.

"Chipmunk? You look more like a grizzly bear," Mac said. "Jesus. Don't you get hot wearing a fur coat in Florida?"

Chipmunk slipped on his fins and duck-walked into the water. He put the snorkel in his mouth and tried to say "Fuck you," but it only came out of the snorkel sounding like a muffled fart. He flopped backward into the water and took a few kicks out into the bright blue water. Mac followed him into the surf.

Mac watched Chipmunk underwater skirting along a rocky ledge, poking his tickle stick under the rocks, and kicking up the sandy bottom. He used one hand to poke under the edge, and with the other carrying a stout fishing net. Suddenly, what appeared to be an enormous cockroach shot backward, missing Chipmunk's net. Instinctively and without any purpose except natural reaction, Mac scooped the scuttering crustacean into his own net. Chipmunk gave the thumbs-up under the surface of the water.

The lobster in Mac's net was fluttering around and trying to escape. Chipmunk switched nets with Mac and transferred the catch to a small mesh bag tethered to his waist. He lifted his head above the surface. Mac poked his head up and spat the snorkel out of his mouth.

"Why doesn't it have claws?" he asked.

"These are warm-water lobster. You're thinking Maine. Cold-water lobster have claws. These are spiny lobster."

"No claws? They look like cockroaches."

"Yeah, locals call 'em bugs."

"That was easy," Mac said. "Let's do it again."

"Let's get two or three more and head back."

Mac nodded, slipped the snorkel back in his mouth, ducked underwater, and continued the expedition.

After filling Chipmunk's sack with four spiny lobsters, the two crawled out of the water and ambled back to the golf cart. Chipmunk tossed a towel over to Mac.

"Not bad for a newbie," Chipmunk said.

"Didn't seem too hard. Water was shallow. Do you do this every day?" Mac toweled himself off.

"No, just a couple of times a month," said Chipmunk. "It's an eight-month season for lobster. But I fish too."

"I have some friends in Aspen that hunt," Mac said. "I usually have a freezer full of venison, but this ain't too bad." He shook out his hair and slid on his flip-flops. "How long have you been in Key West?"

"I guess it's been about eleven years. I went to middle school with Roxy. And high school. We've been friends since seventh grade. I went to culinary school after graduation. Then France for a year," Chipmunk said.

"What did you do in France?"

"Learned how to make sauces pretty much. Bechamel, velouté, *espagnole*, hollandaise—you name it. Oh, and I learned to cook snails."

Chipmunk lit up a joint, took a few puffs, and passed it to Mac.

"So are you a chef?"

"Going to culinary school doesn't make you a chef," said Chipmunk. "Just like going to journalism school doesn't make you a reporter."

"Understood. But did you ever use your degree?"

"My friend and I opened a little breakfast café in Islamorada a few years back. I gave my half to him and his wife for a wedding gift. Then I came down here. I book the bands at the Parrot and manage the bar."

"But you grew up with Roxanne in Palm Beach?"

"If that's your way of asking if my family is rich, the answer is yes. My family is dirty rich."

"That's not exactly what I was asking, but thanks for clearing it up."

"Roxy is a lot like me, man. Money ain't a thing when you grow up with it like we did. Don't let that shit change you, you feel me?"

Mac took another pull from the joint and passed it back. "Yeah, I feel you," he said. "Roxanne tells me she doesn't really date much. You ever meet any of her boyfriends?"

"Not really," Chipmunk said. "She's a complicated girl. I dunno a lot of guys that can hang on to that. No offense."

"What do you mean?"

"Look at her, bro. She's gorgeous. She's rich. That intimidates a lot of guys."

"She doesn't really play off that," Mac said, taking the joint back from Chipmunk.

"How'd you get so lucky, by the way? How did you meet her?"

"I ran into her at a breakfast joint on the beach."

"In Delray Beach."

"Someplace near it. Lantana, maybe."

"And you just walked up to her and said hello?"

"Pretty much," Mac said.

"You've got confidence, man. I'll fucking give you that."

"I like her," Mac said. "She's got something."

Chipmunk dropped the joint and crushed it out with his foot.

"Trust me, brother. I know what you mean," he said.

Mac looked out over the gulf and watched a sailboat drift by. The captain offered a friendly wave. Mac waved back.

"Let's get back and throw these fuckers on the grill," Chipmunk said, hopping into the golf cart.

"Lobster for breakfast," Mac said. "I like it here."

*****

Mac and Chipmunk made a quick stop and picked up two carafes of fresh squeezed orange and grapefruit juice at a rickety joint called Pepe's Café before stopping again for a couple of bottles of cheap champagne. Arriving home, they were greeted by Roxanne laying in a hammock on the front porch of Chipmunk's duplex.

"Hey, rock star," Chipmunk said. "Lobster benny for breakfast."

Mac held up the bottles of champagne. "And mimosas."

"I love tradition," Roxanne said, kicking her feet in the air.

"Mac," Chipmunk said, "go around back and scoop some eggs out of the chicken coop."

"You have a fucking chicken coop?"

"Yeah, there's a wood box on the side. There should be about eight or nine eggs in there. Go grab 'em all."

Mac looked at Roxanne. She smiled. "That's my Chipmunk," she said.

"Oh," Chipmunk said. "Grab a couple of limes from the lime tree too."

Mac opened a small wooden gate and walked into the backyard. He spotted the chicken coop with about four roosters poking around the yard, letting out the occasional wail. Mac peered into the coop and saw two brown hens lazily sitting still. A sign on the coop read "Simon and Theodore." Mac eyed a wooden box resting on the side of the coop, snatched out nine eggs, and walked back into the house, stopping to pull a few golf ball–sized limes from the tree.

Mac walked back into the house through the backdoor. "Your hens have boys' names," he said.

"I'm Alvin, and they're Simon and Theodore," Chipmunk said.

"Giving them boys' names clearly hasn't given them a complex, I see. They're laying eggs all right."

Mac laid the eggs on the countertop. Chipmunk sliced one of Mac's limes in half and went to work on the hollandaise. Roxanne stuck a mimosa in Mac's hand and held one up herself.

"Cheers," she said.

Mac sat down at a breakfast nook. Roxanne sat on his lap. He could smell coffee brewing.

"I gotta say, man. This is amazing. Pulling lobster from the water, eggs and fruit in the backyard. This is paradise," Mac said. "I love it here."

"You fall in love quick," Roxanne said.

"Do I?"

"First with Palm Beach, and now Key West."

"Oh. Is that what you meant?"

"Mac, get up here and stir the hollandaise," Chipmunk said. "And don't stop whisking until I get back."

Roxanne got up, and Mac walked to the stove. "Smells good, chef."

Chipmunk expertly dissected the lobsters, separating the tails and cracking the shells. He went outside to fire them on a grill.

"So," Roxanne said, "I talked to Hanrahan while you guys were out."

"And?"

"A couple of the girls at one of the addresses you gave him told the same story we heard at the coffee shop. Same story the Sadie girl said. Deaver snatches them up for possession, and just like we heard, he tells them he's gonna arrest them or they can check into a halfway house."

"Are any of these girls gonna go on the record?"

"I didn't ask."

"Did Hanrahan go to the houses himself?"

"He drove there with a female staffer at the *Post*. Some younger girl. I don't know her."

"That's smart," Mac said.

"Yeah, Pat said everything is checking out."

"What about Deaver's brother? The diver."

"They just own the real estate together. They're on all the deeds and mortgages together, like you said. But Darrin acts as the landlord. He collects money, he picks up the drug tests, he monitors the girls. He drives them around. He's like a caretaker."

"And he gets them to occasionally relapse, keeping them stuck in the recovery cycle."

"Rehab, relapse, repeat," Roxanne said.

"And Hanrahan was able to confirm through the state registrations all these properties are zoned as halfway houses?"

"Yup."

Chipmunk came back into the house with the grilled lobster tails and ham-fisted some English muffins into a toaster that looked to be eighty years old. Mac stepped away from the hollandaise.

"How'd I do, chef?"

Chipmunk said, "Not bad," and continued whisking the sauce.

He deftly cracked eggs into bubbling water and vinegar to poach and then plated the English muffins—after that, a stack of grilled lobster and a smothering of hollandaise.

Mac sliced up the cantaloupe Chipmunk had rolled down the countertop like a bowling ball. Roxanne set the table. Within minutes, the three of them sat down to an impromptu Key West breakfast of lobster benedict with key lime hollandaise and mimosas with fresh-squeezed juice and melon slices. Mac knew this was probably the best breakfast he could remember having in quite some time. *Maybe even better than that time in New Orleans*, he thought.

Chipmunk hoisted his mimosa in the air. "Here's to lobster tail and champagne. My three favorite things."

*****

Mac and Roxanne took a midday siesta on the porch hammock while Chipmunk strolled off to work later in the afternoon. Mac was still lazily swinging the hammock with one leg when the phone rang. It was a 561 area code—Palm Beach County.

"This is Mac."

An impish voice said, "Hello, darling. How are you?'

It was obviously Patrick Hanrahan from the *Palm Beach Post*.

"Roxanne gave you my number?"

"Of course, she did. Did she give you the early morning update?"

"Yeah. Smart move sending a young girl to the door. Any of the sober house girls going on the record? You talk to that Sadie girl?"

"Not yet, but we can still run with it. The fact-checkers are sold. The property records are strong enough. We're planning to run graphics of the hand-signed deeds we pulled from the tax assessor's office."

"With the Deaver brothers' names on them?"

"Yes, darling. We're going to make a splash."

"That's perfect. Anyone go to Delray PD for a comment?"

"I have a call into the PIO, but I won't hold my breath. We don't need a comment, it's just a formality call. Courtesy, if you will."

"Hey, Pat. Did you talk to my boss at the *Aspen Daily News*?"

"Why, yes, I did."

"Do you mind me asking why you called him?"

"I told you, I've known little David since he first arrived in Aspen. As a society editor, I get invited to Aspen gatherings quite often. It's such a chic crowd. It's too cold for my old bones though, and the people wear too much clothing. A little bundled up for my taste. I prefer to see some skin, if you know what I mean."

Mac slipped out of the hammock and left Roxanne napping. He walked off the porch and down the pebble driveway. "But why did you call him on this story, Pat?"

"Don't worry, darling. Your secret is safe with me."

"What secret is that?"

"How many are you keeping?"

"Pat..."

"I wanted to know who the family you mentioned was that had sent their daughter to rehab out here. I thought maybe I knew them as well. Maybe they knew my niece."

"What did he tell you?"

"He said you came out here to spy on our dear friend Roxanne. It seems you started out with some misinformation. Your story took a shit."

Mac looked back over his shoulder at Roxanne sleeping in the hammock. She looked perfect.

"That's not what I'm doing anymore. I'm not writing about Roxanne."

"Yes, my dear. I am aware of that. It seems that my Aspen prince and Palm Beach princess have clicked like Dorothy's shiny red slippers. I'm not one to shackle a budding romantic tryst…or dirty, hot sex, whatever it is you two are doing."

"I'm going to tell her," Mac said.

"And that's up to you. My lips are sealed. But a little word of advice to you, Bernard."

"Yeah?"

"Don't lie to a fellow reporter. You should know better, my dear."

"What else did Peril have to say?"

"He doesn't like you very much. He said he sent you out here because you're the only staffer they have that isn't either married or geriatric. He also said you'd fuck it up."

"Anything else?"

"Nothing of importance. But he's still that little nasal-voiced Jew I remember. His editorial meetings must be torture. I can't fathom listening to him drone on, sounding like Fran Drescher with a dick."

"Luckily, I'm not invited to those meetings very often, but you've certainly given your description some thought. But look, what else can we do on this story? What do you need from me?" Mac asked.

"Write up a lead and e-mail me some copy. We have enough on our end for tomorrow's paper."

Mac had to think about what day it was. "No shit, this is going in the Sunday paper?"

"Page 1, darling. Headline news."

"That's fantastic."

"Keep it under 250 words and take it easy on the metaphors. I know how you music writers like to get crafty."

"I'll send copy within the next two hours."

"Oh, and how I look forward to it, Bernard. Bye for now."

Mac hung up the phone and walked to the Mustang and grabbed his laptop bag. He walked back onto the porch and slowly rocked Roxanne back and forth in the hammock.

"Hey, sunshine," he said.

"Was that Pat?"

"Yeah. I need to write for a little bit. He needs me to type up some copy. Are you all right here alone for a while?"

"Of course."

"Where should I go write?"

"There's a spot called Blue Heaven by the Hemingway House. You'll feel good there. Good energy. Probably a good place to write."

"Do you want me to bring you anything back?"

"Bring me a puppy."

"A puppy?"

"Something to cuddle with."

"I'll see what I can do." Mac kissed Roxanne on the forehead and walked toward Duvall Street.

*****

Roxanne was right, Mac thought while entering the backyard of Blue Heaven, the place did have good energy. The outdoor wooden bar was inviting, and old sails and tarps were strung across the palm trees to provide shade from the unrelenting Key West sunshine. Mac ordered a Bloody Mary from the bartender who was wearing green-tinted sunglasses and overalls. Mac flipped open his laptop and began banging out some words.

> To: Patrick Hanrahan
> From: Bernard McCaffrey
>
> Delray Beach, the charming "Village by the Sea" in south Palm Beach County, has been experiencing runaway growth of residential housing programs for those recovering from drug addiction, and many of these sober living houses are owned and operated by a local Delray Beach police officer, the *Palm Beach Post* has learned.

"Sober homes" are protected by the Americans with Disabilities Act and also the Fair Housing Act. Federal laws have made it difficult for city officials to limit or otherwise regulate the facilities. However, property records obtained by the *Palm Beach Post* verify six homes zoned by the city as designated sober living homes are owned by Detective Dalton Deaver of the Delray Police Department and his brother, local charter-fishing boat captain, Darrin Deaver.

The national and local epidemic of opioid abuse has created new opportunities for insurance fraud and those looking to exploit loopholes for profit. Under federal law, health-care insurance pays for the costs of recovery. That's led to a boom in residential programs that treat addiction and also growth in deceptive marketing and insurance fraud on behalf of the owners and operators of some of these sober homes. These fraudulent claims have led to a scam known as patient brokering.

These patient brokers—or "junkie hunters," as they're known on the street—tap into insurance money by charging exorbitant rent and receiving kickbacks from outpatient drug treatment centers. Treatment centers and sober homes bill insurance companies not just for rent and drug tests but also for other services. Sometimes, patients can be lured with free scuba diving lessons and chartered boat trips.

According to sources, Detective Deaver has booked several individuals for drug possession and offered to have the charges dropped if these individuals elect to move into one of his sober homes. From there, Deaver is able to bill the insurance companies and collect a handsome profit.

Mac read over his copy. Satisfied, he emailed the attachment to Hanrahan, assuming he would add his own copy and flush out the details and add some quotes from the girls living in Deaver's sober home. Mac watched more roosters amble around the outdoor restaurant. Several cats were strewn about the backyard, sunning their fat bellies and lying about.

"Hey," Mac said to the bartender. "What's your name?"

"Larry."

"How about another Bloody Mary, Larry?"

"You got it."

Mac motioned to the felines. "What's with the cats? Not that I care myself, but aren't they a health-code violation?"

"I dunno, man. I've worked here for twenty years, and I don't think we've been cited."

"Whose cats are they?"

"Ernest Hemingway's."

"You do know he's been dead for a while, right, Larry?"

"Of course. In 1961 in Ketchum, Idaho. You don't live in Key West without becoming an amateur Hemingway biographer."

Mac sipped his fresh Bloody Mary. "So about the cats?"

"Hemingway had a bunch of cats at his place down the street. None of them were fixed. They just kept having litters of kittens."

"So now all the cats in Key West are related to the Hemingway cats? Is there some sort of feline genealogist on the island?"

"Not exactly. But Hemingway had polydactyl cats. It's a genetically inherited characteristic."

"What the fuck is a polydactyl cat?"

"They usually have six or seven toes."

"Is this a true story?"

"Indeed."

"Ernest Hemingway bred mutant cats?"

"I mean, when you put it like that..."

"Roosters and malformed cats. This place definitely has its quirks."

"First time in Key West?"

"First time in Florida."

"Yeah," Larry said, taking a deep breath. "No place else like Key West."

*****

Mac did some shopping on Duval Street before heading back to Chipmunk's duplex. He picked up another Hawaiian shirt for himself and a stuffed bulldog plush toy for Roxanne. After all, Mac thought, she did ask for him to return with a puppy.

Mac found Roxanne just where he had left her, swinging gently in the hammock.

"Here's your puppy," he said, tossing the stuffed animal in her lap. She gave it a squeeze.

"He's cute. What's his name?"

"You tell me."

Roxanne looked at the toy animal. "He looks like Winston Churchill."

Mac took a closer look. "I agree," he said.

He climbed into the hammock alongside Roxanne. She cuddled against his warm body.

"Did you finish writing?" she asked.

"I sent Hanrahan the story lead and some extra copy. He should be able to bring it home."

"Did I hear you say Pat wants to publish this story tomorrow?"

"Yes. He said it's going on page 1."

"Did you tell your bosses back in Aspen?"

"What do you mean?"

"It sounds like you've given up on the story you were supposed to be writing."

"There's probably something I should tell you," Mac said. "I don't think my boss back in Aspen is happy with the job I've done here anyway."

"What makes you say that?"

"He cut off my expense account."

"Do you have to go back to Colorado?"

"He also kinda fired me."

Roxanne sat up a little bit. "Kinda fired you? What's that mean?"

"He said, 'You're fired.'"

"How is that *kinda* fired? That sounds like, fired, fired."

"Technically, he can't fire me while I'm on an assignment. But I think when I get back to Aspen, it'll become more official."

"Does that mean you're moving to Florida?"

"Maybe. But in the present, it means I don't have a place to stay and my company credit card is canceled."

"I have plenty of money."

"That's an understatement, but I'm not that kinda guy. I don't want to take advantage."

"Just stay with me at the Sun Dek for a few days. Is your flight open-ended?"

"It is."

"So fuck it," Roxanne said. She kicked her feet in the air. "You have nothing to worry about."

Mac agreed with the ethos. "Yeah, fuck it."

"Why did they kill the story?"

Mac said, "I think I might have killed the story."

SUNDAY

Mac spent the rest of Saturday emailing story copy back and forth with Patrick Hanrahan, hashing out the story slated for page 1 in the Sunday edition of the *Palm Beach Post*. The girls he had shaken loose from the halfway houses provided all the color the story needed, and while Mac hadn't seen the final edit, the story was strong and was certain to pull the tails of those pussycats at the Delray Beach Police Department. At least that's how Hanrahan phrased it.

After throwing their bags in the back of the Mustang, Mac joined Roxanne and Chipmunk on the porch for formal goodbyes.

"Thanks for the hospitality," Mac said. He stuck out his hand, which Chipmunk swatted it away and delivered a crushing bear hug instead, lifting Mac off his feet in the process.

"You did good catching those lobsters, buddy. You take care of my friend here."

"Are you kidding? She's taking care of me."

Roxanne and Chipmunk embraced before Mac and Roxanne departed in the Mustang, trying to get a jump on the weekend traffic heading north out of the Keys. They stopped at Cow Key to put the top down and get gas before speeding off on the four-hour drive back to Delray Beach.

The distance between Key West and Key Largo is about a hundred miles, and the route is famously peppered with mile markers that have become more or less iconic to those who frequent the drive. The journey is a puddle jump between islands, basically an archipelago connected by narrow bridges. Driving north, the Atlantic Ocean lies to the east, and the Gulf of Mexico to the west. The narrow strip of concrete cutting through the islands acts as a barrier between the bodies of water. It was a remarkable sight to behold, thought Mac, as he skipped the Mustang over the small islands.

"Where do you want to stop and grab the paper?" he asked. "It's probably on newsstands down here by now."

"Let's stop in Islamorada. It's pretty much the halfway mark between Key West and Delray," Roxanne said. She clutched her stuffed animal toy. "Winston here will probably need to take a bathroom break."

"I'm excited to see the layout of the story," Mac said.

"Are you nervous?" Roxanne asked.

"About what?"

"About the Delray Beach police looking for your ass when we get back. After they see the story."

"I don't have a byline, and I don't work for the *Palm Beach Post*. The only thing tying me to the story would be assumption."

"I know you journalists think cops are stupid, but I'm pretty sure Deaver is going to put it together."

"I have to think after this story breaks, there's going to be an internal investigation. Deaver will probably be put on administrative leave until the department can figure out if what he's doing is at all legal, which it's really not. At that point, Deaver will probably get fired. If he still wants to be a cop, it wouldn't be in his best interest to harass me. He won't score any points provoking me or anyone at the *Palm Beach Post*."

"What about his brother?"

"Darrin the Diver? What about him?"

"I got started with all of this myself to find out who got Juliette to relapse. It sounds like Dalton Deaver is going to take the fall for this, but what about his brother?"

"I'm pretty sure the IRS is going to shutter the halfway houses and maybe even repossess his boat. We're cutting off his finances. He'll get what's coming too."

"I'd still like to know what happened with Juliette."

"We can still talk to him. Although if he lawyers up, which he probably will, I don't think he'll be in a very talkative mood."

"I guess."

"Don't pout. We're putting these fuckers out of business. I think that's justice, don't you?"

"I just wonder if Juliette would still be alive if she never came here for rehab. Maybe if her parents sent her someplace else instead of South Florida."

"We're shutting down six halfway houses. I think that's a start. I think Juliette would be happy about that," Mac said.

*****

Mac stopped at the 7-Eleven in Islamorada and picked up two cups of coffee and two copies of the *Palm Beach Post*. Roxanne waited in the car. There, on page 1, above the fold in bold letters showed: "DELRAY BEACH POLICE DEPARTMENT SOBER HOUSING SWINDLE."

Mac returned to the Mustang as Roxanne was bent over the car, stretching her long legs. She looked effortlessly sexy. He gave her a copy of the paper and a Styrofoam cup of coffee, and they both read the story together. Mac finished reading first and waited for Roxanne to catch up.

"Wow," she said. "Those guys are fucked."

"Hanrahan really put this thing together."

Roxanne folded the paper closed. "You got this story, Mac. Take the credit," she said.

Mac began reading the story a second time.

"There's gotta be a follow-up, right?" Roxanne asked.

"Absolutely. This story has legs. Now my guess is Hanrahan waits to see what the brass do at Delray PD. Then the story becomes the investigation. The IRS is probably going to come after the Deavers to see if they've been claiming all that rent money as income, and the insurance companies are going to start going through billing record addresses. The Deavers are going to get audited. Probably hit with back taxes, maybe evasion."

Roxanne asked, "Do you think they'll go to jail?"

"I don't think Detective Deaver is going to the company picnic this year."

Mac's phone vibrated in his pocket. He took the phone out and looked at the caller ID. "It's Hanrahan," he said to Roxanne. He answered the phone, "We just read the story now."

"What did you think, darling?"

"I think we nailed it."

"I haven't *nailed* anything in quite some time. But this story belongs to you, Bernard."

"Has there been a response? Any word from the feds?"

"It's too early, my dear, and it's a Sunday. I haven't been to the office yet. However, I'm at a newsstand on the island in Palm Beach looking at something you might be very, very interested in. Where are you two?"

Mac looked around. "We're in Islamorada, I think. At a 7-Eleven. We just picked up the paper."

"I think you ought to go back inside and look for a copy of the *National Enquirer*," Hanrahan said. "See if they have it there by now. It just hit this news-stand today."

Mac started walking back into the gas station as Roxanne continued reading the *Post* story again. She sipped her coffee.

"The *National Enquirer*? Why?"

"Because you're on the cover, honey."

Mac said, "Yeah, right."

"With Roxanne. You're both on the cover of the *National Enquirer*, Bernard."

Mac walked up to a spinning magazine rack inside the 7-Eleven and gave it a twirl. "Funny. We're on the cover of the *National Enquirer*?"

He kept spinning the rack.

"Keep looking. I'm not joking with you."

Mac found the *Globe* and *Star* Magazine before his eyes landed on the *National Enquirer*. He slipped it out of the sleeve and held the tabloid up to eye level.

"Fuck me," he said.

"Sounds like you found it."

There, on the front page of the *National Enquirer*, was the headline: "Wasting Away in Margaritaville: Conrad Harvey Daughter Drunk and Disturbed after Daddy's Death."

Underneath the headline were two pictures. One was of Mac and Roxanne sitting poolside at the Marriott, showing Roxanne pressing her signature margarita to her lips with Mac sitting next to her, smiling obliviously. The second photograph was more familiar. It was the picture Mac had taken of Roxanne outside the Crossroads Club, entering a Narcotics Anonymous meeting.

"What the fuck is this?" Mac said, flipping the tabloid open. "Roxanne isn't gonna like this. This isn't good at all. This is bad."

"I certainly don't think she'll be amused," Hanrahan said. "Is this your doing, Bernard?"

"Absolutely not."

Mac flipped through the pages. The article was a two-page spread at the fold. It was only a few hundred words, but the photos told a story.

"Do you know where the photographs came from? Did you know our friend was being followed by paparazzi?" Hanrahan asked.

"It's not paparazzi. It's a private investigator."

"So you do have more secrets, don't you?"

"This is a big deal," Mac said. "What am I supposed to tell her?"

"Tell her she's a tabloid baby."

"Tabloid baby?"

"Page 1 splash. Roxanne Harvey is this season's tabloid baby. She's all the rage."

"This isn't cute."

Mac paid for the *Enquirer* and walked outside and stared at Roxanne sitting in the Mustang holding Winston Churchill and sipping her coffee. She looked over and smiled. She had just applied lipstick again.

"Tabloid baby, huh."

"She's a tabloid baby, baby."

"Fuck," Mac said.

*****

Roxanne hit Mac in the face with Winston Churchill. "You're a fucking liar!"

"Not exactly," he responded.

"How are you not a liar? You didn't come to Florida to write about the sober homes. You came to spy on me. You came here to write about my dad." She swung the plush toy again.

"Sometimes a news story can take twists and turns. It's a very complicated matter, Roxanne."

"But you were sent here to write about me, and you didn't tell me. That doesn't sound too complicated."

"Omission isn't lying."

"*Yes, it is!*"

"I'm sorry. It wasn't a lie. It was more of a ruse."

"A ruse? You lied."

Mac was still navigating the Mustang on US 1, heading out of the Keys, nothing but blue sky in every direction. Roxanne was flipping through the *National Enquirer*, its pages fluttering in the wind as Mac kept driving north.

Roxanne began reading aloud. "*Roxanne Harvey, daughter of recently deceased television icon Conrad Harvey, is drowning her sorrows in bottomless margaritas while simultaneously seeking help through Alcoholic Anonymous meetings and the comfort of a new mystery man,"* she read. *"And friends fear her relapse into sex and booze could lead to a tragic end, similar to what befell her late mother Suzette Cox, who died of a drug and alcohol overdose in 1994.'* What the fuck, Mac? You're a mystery man? They're talking about my mom?"

"I didn't write that."

Roxanne kept reading. "This is crazy. This is garbage."

"I know. I'm a way-better writer. I'd never write such poor copy."

"Is there anything else you'd like to tell me? Now's the fucking time."

"What do you want to know?"

"Everything. Start with the beginning and try and avoid omissions this time."

Mac tried to recap the best he could. "I got to work on Monday, and my page editor, Charlie, and I got called into an office…"

Roxanne wasn't interested in long explanations, but she had questions. "Who wanted you to do this? Why did you come to Florida?"

Mac tried to focus on the road. "I got called into the editor's office last Monday."

Roxanne said, "Continue."

"I'm trying," Mac said. "He said the paper wanted to run something about you since your father had a connection to Aspen. That guy Leaky, the guy that got hit by the train, he called his sister at the *Durango Herald.*"

"The *Durango Herald?*"

"Yeah, it's another small town daily. His sister called the *Aspen Daily News*."

"What's this have to do with me?"

"The *Aspen Daily News* heard you were going to AA meetings. They thought since your father was an Aspen figurehead and holds water in Summit County that it would fit into the editorial lineup. They thought it was newsworthy. For what it's worth, I told them it wasn't."

"And they sent you here to spy on me?"

"I guess."

"What the fuck, Mac?"

"Listen to me, please. Once I saw you and once I talked to Leaky, I knew you weren't an addict. I also heard about the sober house scams and insurance fraud that's destroying South Florida. I wanted to help you with Juliette."

"That's bullshit. You wanted to get in my pants and squeeze a job at the *Palm Beach Post* since you fucked up your assignment."

"No, that's not it at all. And I didn't fuck up my assignment."

"Mac, I'm on the cover of the *National Enquirer*!"

"So am I."

"But it's your fault!"

"I don't know how this happened. I don't know anyone at the *National Enquirer*."

Roxanne continued staring at the tabloid.

"Is there anything else you're not telling me? Anything else I should know about?"

"Well," Mac said, "I did take that photo of you outside of the Crossroads Club."

Roxanne held up the tabloid and pointed to the photograph. "This one?" she asked.

Mac glanced over while trying to keep his eyes on the road. "Yeah."

Roxanne slapped Mac with the newspaper. "Asshole!"

"I emailed the photographs to the *Aspen Daily News*. Now I'm guessing they sold it to the *Enquirer*."

"Why?"

"Well, I'm gonna find out."

"Anything else?"

"Yeah…you're being followed."

"I'm being followed?"

"Yeah, by Eli Stransky."

"Who the fuck is Eli Stransky? Jesus Christ, Mac."

"He's a private investigator."

"A private investigator? He's following me?"

Roxanne looked over her shoulder.

"He's not following you right now," said Mac.

"Who is he? Why's he following me?"

"He works for some estate attorneys in Palm Beach. Let me ask you a question now: has your father's estate been settled?"

"I don't really know. The attorneys are handling that."

"Are you the only surviving heir?"

"As far as I know."

"Are you getting everything?"

"I don't know, Mac. My father just died three weeks ago. My friend just died six weeks ago. And now I'm on the cover of the *National* fucking *Enquirer*. I'm sorry if I'm a little confused right now."

"I get it. When we get back to Delray Beach, I'll track down this Stransky guy and shake him down."

"You're gonna shake him down?"

"I'm going to find out why he's following you, and I'm going to find out how this all ended up in the tabloids."

"Did you use me, Mac?"

"Absolutely not. I quit my job for you."

"I thought you said you got fired?"

"Semantics."

"This is pretty shitty, Mac."

"I'll take care of it. I'll fix this."

Roxanne shook her head in distrust. "Is that it? Anything else you want to clear up?" she asked.

"Yeah," Mac said. "There's something else." He looked over at her. She continued staring ahead. Mac continued, "My father isn't dead."

"You lied about that to get some sympathy, didn't you? That's disgusting."

"I was trying to find common ground. We have so little in common."

"Is he at least sick?"

"No. He's a retired college professor. Now he bets on the horses in Saratoga and plays internet poker," Mac said.

"What about your mom?"

"She paints clowns."

"Clowns?"

"Yeah. And landscapes. It's paint by number, so don't get too excited."

Roxanne managed a small, caustic chuckle. "Can I trust you from now on?"

Mac accelerated the Mustang out of Key Largo and over Jewfish Creek toward Homestead, Florida.

He said, "Absolutely."

*****

Roxanne and Mac beat the Sunday traffic and arrived back in South Florida a little after 1:00 p.m. Mac parked in a guest spot at Roxanne's rental at the Sun Dek and dragged the luggage upstairs and into her unit.

Roxanne quickly undressed and got into the shower. Mac stepped outside and phoned the *Aspen Daily News*. Peril answered his office phone.

"You slippery shit," Mac said. "You sold me out."

Mac heard a familiar annoying voice. "Oh, hello, Bernard."

"Don't call me that, asshole. You sold me out. You burned me."

"I didn't sell you out. You ran up an absurd bill on the *Aspen Daily News* expense account. That got *me* into shit with the publishers, so I had to dig us out of the shit. And I don't like being buried in shit in the first place."

"You sold the story to the *National Enquirer*? You sold them a photograph I took and without my permission?"

"Those photographs belong to the *Aspen Daily News,* not you. You captured that image while under the employ of this newspaper. You also took the photo with a camera you stole from the photo department."

Mac corrected him. "Borrowed. I borrowed the camera."

"Doesn't matter, Bernard. I had to recover the funds you wasted fucking around out there."

"Where did you get the other photos? Where did they get the photos of me?"

"Now you're just playing dumb."

Mac's blood pressure was rising. "Stop calling me Bernard, you nasal-voiced fuck. I'm going to come back to Aspen and choke you out in front of that entire newsroom. I am going to piss on your desk."

"Well, before you go to the airport, I should let you know that your open-ended return flight has been canceled. If you wanna get back here to clean out your desk, it's on your own dime."

"Did you get the photos from Stransky, or did he contact the *Enquirer* himself?"

"Does it really matter anymore?"

"Did you talk to Stransky? Why is he following Roxanne?"

"I guess you're not the hotshot reporter you thought you were, now are you?"

"Fuck you."

"Stick to live music, asshole."

The phone went dead before Mac could respond.

Mac walked back into the apartment. Roxanne had gotten out of the shower and was getting dressed. The *Palm Beach Post* and *National Enquirer* were both splashed out on the king-sized bed. Mac picked up the *Post*.

"What do you want me to do, Roxanne?"

She was putting in earrings. "About what?"

"Do you want me to follow up on the *Palm Beach Post* story with Hanrahan, or do you want me to try and put an end to this *National Enquirer* coverage?"

"I really don't want to keep seeing my picture in a fucking supermarket tabloid. I've managed to live my life fairly anonymously up to this point, and I think I'd like that to continue. Did you find anything out?"

"I found out my boss back in Aspen sold the story to the *National Enquirer* to cover the expenses of my trip out here."

"That sounds really petty."

"Peril is the poster child of petty. Always has been."

"Your editor sold pictures to the *National Enquirer*? Isn't that some sort of ethics violation?"

"Journalism has lost a lot of its principles lately. Besides, David Peril doesn't have any ethics."

Mac dropped the paper back on the bed and inched close to Roxanne, who was applying her makeup in the mirror.

"I didn't use you for anything," he said. "I tried to keep you out of this as soon as we met."

"I know."

"I had no idea this was going to happen."

Roxanne turned around and faced him. She grabbed his face with two hands.

"You lied to me. Don't do it again."

"I won't. In fact, I don't even want to leave you alone right now, but I'm going to go track down this Stransky guy and find out what's happening. I need you to do me a favor."

"What's that?"

"Call your father's estate attorney and ask if he's been contacted by anyone at Walker, Bisset and Turnhill."

"Who are they?"

"They're the lawyers that employ the services of Eli Stransky."

"It's Sunday. I don't know if I'll get anyone on the phone."

"Just get a message out to them."

Mac grabbed his car keys and sunglasses.

"What are you going to do?" asked Roxanne.

"I have Stransky's home address. I'm going there to get some information."

"You don't want me to come with you?"

"No, sit this one out. I'll be back later."

"Is it safe?"

"I didn't receive the Congressional Medal of Honor by avoiding conflict. I'm brave, remember?"

Roxanne smiled. Mac kissed her and slipped on his flip-flops. He was wearing his new Hawaiian shirt, the one he bought in Key West. It had lobsters on it.

*****

Eli Stransky lived on a dead-end street in west Delray Beach, about fifteen miles from the Sun Dek. Mac drove down the desolate street and spotted the familiar Volkswagen parked in the driveway. The end of the street was a cul-de-sac, peppered with only a couple of small homes. Stransky's single-family ranch-style house was the last house on the right. The screen door was partially open, but Stransky wasn't outside.

Mac pulled a U-turn and parked at the end of the street behind a cargo van. He stepped out of the Mustang, one flip-flop after the other, and walked toward the Stransky residence, talking to himself and trying to psych himself up.

Stay away from my girlfriend, you asshole, he said to himself.

Mac shook a fist in the air. "Keep away from my girl, you piece of shit," he said. "Hey, Stransky, why don't you leave my girl alone before I fuck you up?"

As Mac approached the house, he heard the screen door from Stransky's porch slam shut. He watched as the man ambled down his driveway and opened his mailbox. Mac kept walking, slowly getting closer. When he was within six feet, he yelled, "Hey, Stransky!"

With one hurried motion, Stransky frisbeed his mail at Mac, pulled a small caliber pistol from his waistband, and pointed it directly at Mac's face.

"Stop, asshole," he said. "Florida is a stand-your-ground state. Do you know what that means?"

Mac hesitated. "Yes," he said.

"What does it mean?"

"I was lying…I don't know what that means."

"It means if you approach me aggressively and I feel threatened, I can shoot you in the face," Stransky said. "And it will be justified."

"Do you really think this is the first time I've had a gun stuck in my face?"

"Yes, I do."

"Okay, fair enough. It is."

"What do you want?"

"My name is Bernard McCaffrey."

"Yeah, I fucking know who you are. What do you want?"

"You mean other than having you get that gun out of my face?"

"Why are you here, McCaffrey, on my private property?"

"Why don't you put the gun down, man? This isn't a Tarantino movie."

Stransky didn't flinch. "What do you want?"

"Why are you following Roxanne Harvey?"

"I was hired to. It's a job."

"I saw you at the Marriott. Did you sell those photographs to the *National Enquirer*? Was that part of the job?"

"That part was extracurricular."

"Why did Walker, Bisset and Turnhill hire you to follow Roxanne?"

"Why don't you just walk away, McCaffrey? Get the fuck out of here."

"Look, man," said Mac, "I'm just trying to find out why a group of estate attorneys hired you to follow my girlfriend."

"Your girlfriend?"

"Whatever, man. Can you put the gun down?"

"Look, Romeo, you think you know who that girl's father is, don't you?"

"Was."

"What?"

"Was. Who her father *was*. Conrad Harvey died almost three weeks ago. What the fuck is it with you people and your inability to distinguish past and present tense?"

"You definitely don't know who her father is."

"What are you talking about? Conrad Harvey is Roxanne's father."

"No, he's not," Stransky said. "Conrad Harvey isn't Roxanne Harvey's biological father."

"Excuse me?"

"Her real father…her biological father…he's in France."

"What?"

"Go talk to Lucien Bisset."

"What are you taking about? Her biological father?"

Before Stransky could answer, Mac heard screeching tires and saw a white blur from the corner of his eye. This was followed by Eli Stransky's body catapulting fifteen feet in the air and crashing down, shattering the windshield of his Volkswagen. His pistol fell at Mac's feet, which he instinctively picked up. Roxanne Harvey's Maserati was now parked where Stransky had been standing a split second earlier. She stepped out of the car.

"What the fuck?" Mac said.

Roxanne looked at Stransky's body as it slid off the car and hit the driveway with a thump. She seemed oddly collected considering the immediate circumstance. "Do you think he's dead?" she asked.

"What the fuck?" Mac repeated.

"He was pointing a gun at you."

"So you hit him with a car? This isn't a fucking video game, Roxanne. This isn't *Grand Theft Auto.* This is real life."

"Is he dead?"

"I'm not dead," Stransky mumbled. "The cops are on their way."

He lifted up his cell phone over his head. He was bleeding from somewhere. Mac looked at Roxanne.

"What the fuck?" Mac said again.

"I followed you," she said.

"Yes, I see that."

"Are you okay?"

"Am I okay? You just hit somebody with a car."

"It looked like he deserved it."

"No, I didn't," Stransky said, rolling over onto his back. "My fucking leg is broken."

Roxanne walked over and kicked him. "Why are you following me, asshole?"

Stransky laughed.

Roxanne kicked him again. "Why are you following me, shit head?"

Police sirens wailed in the background. Mac tossed the pistol into Roxanne's car and pulled her away from the crippled private investigator. He embraced her just as police cruisers rounded the dead-end street, speeding toward Stransky's driveway.

*****

"So let me get this straight," the police officer said. "The Stransky fella pulled a gun on you."

"Yes," Mac said. He and Roxanne sat in the cop's office, trying to cooperate.

"And you hit him with a Maserati?"

"That's correct," Roxanne said.

The cop leaned back in his chair. The nameplate on his desk said "Officer Steven Rohrbach." He let out a deep sigh. "This is some bullshit I didn't need today."

"Look," Roxanne said. "We went to his house to discuss some work-related matters. Eli Stransky is a private investigator."

"I know Stransky. He used to be a cop in New Jersey. Got into some trouble up there, from what I've heard. Not a real popular guy as far as I know."

"Here or in New Jersey?" Mac asked.

"Both."

"So you know him?"

"I know of him."

"He's an asshole," Roxanne said. "Did you know that?"

"Being an asshole doesn't change the legality of running him over with a Maserati."

"He pulled his piece on me," Mac said.

"His piece?"

"His gat."

"His gat?"

"His gun. Whatever, man. He pulled his gun, and he stuck it in my face."

"And she hit him with her car?"

"*Yes*," Roxanne and Mac said simultaneously.

Officer Rohrbach scribbled on a pad of paper. "So you'll be claiming self-defense on this, I assume?"

"I'll do whatever my lawyer suggests," Roxanne said. "Am I being charged with anything?"

"You're at least getting charged with reckless endangerment for now. I'm not sure what Stransky plans to pursue."

"How is he?" Mac asked. "Stransky."

"He's at Bethesda now. Broken leg and collar-bone. Some cracked ribs."

"Is he taking visitors?"

"Why? Are you gonna bring him some fucking balloons?"

"Our conversation was interrupted."

"That's one way to put it."

"Where's my car?" Roxanne asked.

"Impound. Same with the Mustang."

Mac looked out the officer's window and noticed a couple of news vans and a crowd of press corps milling around.

"What's with the media?" he asked.

Officer Rohrbach leaned back and twisted the blinds shut. "It's a circus," he said. "We got press all over the place today."

"Why?" Roxanne asked.

"I take it you didn't read the *Palm Beach Post* this morning? Nobody reads the paper anymore."

"I was busy," she said.

Mac glanced at Roxanne and smirked. She smiled at him.

"What was in the *Post*?" Mac asked.

"Apparently, one of our less scrupulous detectives had some questionable streams of income. Press is all over it."

"What was he doing? Was it legal?"

"I don't know entirely. Insurance fraud, I think. Something along those lines. I didn't read the whole article. The chief is going to brief the whole department later."

"Is he getting arrested?"

"He's been put on administrative leave. He's actually down the hall getting grilled by the chief and a couple of guys from the district attorney's office. That's why the press is outside. They're waiting for an official statement."

"That looked like a lot of press."

"Don't be jealous, they're here for you too," the cop said.

"For who?"

"For her," he said, motioning to Roxanne.

"Me?" said Roxanne.

"Are you two living on a different planet? You're on the cover of the *National Enquirer*, for Christ's sake. And you just hit a guy with your car. You're Conrad Harvey's kid. You didn't think the press would jump on this?"

"You know who she is?" Mac asked. "You don't strike me as a tabloid reader."

"Of course I know who she is. I just wrote her ticket."

"That's not what I meant."

"You two really need to turn on a TV. Get online or something."

Roxanne got up and reopened the blinds and looked out over the swarm of press. "They're here for me?"

"Some of them are, yeah."

"Why?"

"You're, uh, what's the word my daughter uses? *Trending*. That's it. You're trending right now."

"I'm trending? I'm not famous."

"You're on the cover of the *National Enquirer*. You're famous as far as they're concerned."

"How'd they know I'm here?"

"This is a police department. This isn't the best place for secrets."

"They think I'm a drunk that just ran somebody over with my car. This is fucking perfect." Roxanne looked over at Mac, not as lovingly as before. "I wonder how this happened?"

Mac changed the subject. "Are we done here, Officer?" he asked.

The cop scribbled on some papers and handed them to Roxanne, who stuffed them in her handbag without looking at them.

"I'd read those if I were you, Ms. Harvey. You have a court appearance in a few weeks. I'm sure your lawyer will postpone it, but I'd definitely seek counsel. I don't know if Stransky has insurance, but his medical bills won't be cheap. With your net worth, you can probably expect to get sued."

"Thank you," she said. "I'm sure my lawyers can handle a lowlife like Eli Stransky."

Officer Rohrbach led Roxanne and Mac through a hallway, into a main lobby, and then down an adjacent hallway. Mac looked at the police-officer portraits lining the walls. They walked by a room with glass windows, and Mac glanced inside. He halted and pulled Roxanne by the back of her shirt.

"Look," he said.

Roxanne looked through the window. There, sitting across from three guys in suits, was a very nervous-looking Detective Deaver.

"That's Deaver right there," Mac said.

Roxanne banged on the glass. Deaver looked up, and the men in suits all turned their heads.

Roxanne extended her middle finger emphatically and tapped it against the glass. Mac offered a friendly wave and toothy grin. Deaver pointed and started to say something.

Mac continued walking, rounded the corner, and smacked right into Officer Morris.

"Just the scumbag I was looking for," the cop said.

"Oh, hey, I just saw your boyfriend back there. He looked upset. Did you forget your anniversary again?"

Morris grabbed Mac by the collar. Officer Rohrbach stepped between them.

"What's the problem here? Back up, Morris."

"This guy is wanted for questioning."

"For what?"

"The guy that got hit by the train outside O'Connor's. The Indian guy."

"This guy here? What's he got to do with it?"

"He's a suspect."

"Suspected of what?"

"Deaver wants him to provide a statement on Tuesday. He was drunk with the guy the night he died."

"So what?" Rohrbach said.

"So Deaver thinks he's a suspect."

"Again, Morris, suspected of what?"

"Possible homicide."

"Homicide?"

"That's what Deaver said."

"I don't think Deaver's gonna be handling his cases anymore. I'll ask the chief to parlay that case over to me. Sounds like some bullshit."

Morris tried again to intervene. "I'm telling you. Deaver thinks this guy pushed the Indian in front of the train."

"What's the motive?" Rohrbach asked. "I've heard nothing about this. I don't think any of Deaver's cases are being taken as genuine right now, as a matter of fact. So back away, Morris."

"He's wanted for questioning. He's supposed to provide a statement on Tuesday."

"A deposition doesn't mean I'm a suspect, you dimwit," Mac said.

Morris lunged at Mac, who slipped away and slid behind the other officer.

"Does the chief know anything about this at all?" Rohrbach asked.

Roxanne reached into her purse and retrieved Mac's digital recorder. She pressed play.

> *"I want you to stop investigating my real-estate investments and kill your pathetic little newspaper story. Go back to your mountain town and pretend like you've never heard of Delray Beach."*
>
> *"And if I don't, you're going to falsify murder charges against me? I'm pretty sure that's extortion, and*

in most states, even Florida, extortion is a crime."

"Not as punishable as a murder charge."

"I don't know how happy my editor is going to be if I don't have a story to print. That's kind of an important element when it comes to publishing a newspaper."

"That's not my problem. But whatever you write, if you mention my name or my brother's name, I will have you extradited back to Florida, and I will charge you with murdering Leonard Lapahie. And that's after I have Morris here stick a soldering iron up your ass."

Morris stopped and backed away.

"I'm gonna ask again, Morris. Does the chief even know about this investigation?" Rohrbach asked.

"Sounds like you two have a lot to talk about," Mac said.

"I told you. It's Deaver's case," Morris said. "He's working that case."

"That sounded like blackmail to me, Morris."

"It's not my case. That wasn't my voice."

"Get out of the way," Rohrbach said, pushing Mac and Roxanne past Morris and toward the front door. "I'll deal with you later. And Ms. Harvey, try and keep your car between the lines."

"Thank you, Officer," she said.

"Take it easy, Morris," Mac said. "And go fuck yourself."

*****

Cameras flashed as Mac and Roxanne made their way down the concrete precinct steps. Reporters barked questions and rushed Roxanne. Mac tried to shield her.

"Roxanne, were you driving drunk? Have you been charged with a DUI?" one asked.

"Who's your boyfriend, Roxanne? Did he know your father?" asked another.

"Are you an addict, Ms. Harvey? Are you an alcoholic?"

Mac wrapped his arm around Roxanne and stiff-armed a few people out of the way.

"We don't have a car," Roxanne said. "They're both in impound."

"We need to get out of here," Mac said.

He felt a tug on the back of his Hawaiian shirt. He turned around.

"Hello, my tabloid babies," said a familiar voice. It was Patrick Hanrahan.

"*Pat!*" Roxanne shrieked. "Thank god."

Hanrahan was wearing a pink dress shirt with navy blue pants and a straw boater hat. "Come on, darlings. I'm parked in the courthouse garage," he said. He flipped his keys to Mac. "You drive."

Mac pushed through the reporters and out onto SW 1st Street, turning south toward the parking garage.

"I thought they were here for the rehab story," Roxanne said.

"They were," Hanrahan said. "That's why I'm here. There's supposed to be a press briefing. The chief is going to make a statement. But then we were informed the beautiful and troubled alcoholic daughter of Conrad Harvey just ran someone over in an Italian sports car."

"This is crazy," Mac said.

"This is your fault," Roxanne barked. "All your fault, Mac. And I'm not an alcoholic, Pat."

"Oh, darling, I know. *I'm* the alcoholic of this troop."

Ducking into the parking garage, Hanrahan nodded to a new Lincoln Town Car. "That's us."

The three of them climbed into the car. Hanrahan shuffled into the backseat. Mac started the car. The radio blasted to life.

"I did it myyyyyyy waaayyyyyyyyy…"

Mac turned off Sinatra. "Sorry, Frank," he said. "Where are we going?"

"Bethesda Hospital," Roxanne said. "I still want to talk to Stransky."

Mac said, "That's probably not the best idea."

"Why not? Is there something else you're not telling me?"

Mac pulled out onto Atlantic Avenue. "I'm not sure what Stransky was trying to tell me before you played bumper cars with him, but it sounded like something that might not be easy to hear."

Roxanne asked, "What are you talking about?"

"Stransky. He said something before you hit him with the car."

"Oh, just spill it, Bernard," Hanrahan said.

"He said something about your father," Mac said.

"What about him?"

"Something about him being in France."

"Last I checked, he was in an urn back at the ranch in Wellington."

"Not Conrad," Mac said. "Your biological father."

*****

Bethesda Hospital was only two miles away from the police station. Surprisingly, the desk clerk didn't hesitate to provide the room number for Eli Stransky, despite the fact that Roxanne had caused his current residency.

Mac, Roxanne, and Hanrahan entered room 205 to find him laid up with his leg in a sling and wrapped in a cast. His face was bruised. He was watching TV.

Mac walked in first. "Jesus," he said. "You look like you got hit by a car."

"Oh, not you again. Where's my gun?"

208

"Stransky, this is Roxanne Harvey," Mac said.

"I know who she is. You're on the TV, by the way. Care to watch?"

They looked up at the mounted television. TMZ was showing the *National Enquirer* photographs and interviewing some talking heads. The television was on mute, but it was obvious who they were talking about.

"I can turn up the volume if you want," Stransky said.

Roxanne snatched the remote and switched off the TV. "Why were you following me, Mr. Stransky?"

"Are you gonna hit me with your car again if I don't tell you?"

Roxanne said, "Maybe."

"Look, I got a job a couple of weeks ago for some lawyers I occasionally do some work for."

"Walker, Bisset and Turnhill," Mac said.

"Yeah. Lucien Bisset called me. He wanted me to locate Roxanne Harvey."

Roxanne asked, "Why?"

"Walker, Bisset and Turnhill have an office in France. Lucien works both sides of the pond. He's got a client named Jean Laurent. He's a chef in Paris, apparently. That's what he tells me."

"Why are you following me, Mr. Stransky?" Roxanne asked again.

"Who the fuck is Jean Laurent?" Mac asked.

"Originally, I was just supposed to track you down. You weren't living at the family ranch in Wellington, and we didn't know where you were. I noticed you got a parking ticket in Delray Beach, so I started looking for your car there. Nice Maserati, by the way. I finally saw you crossing the tracks on Lake Ida Road. I followed you back to the Sun Dek in Ocean Ridge. Found out you were staying there. I gave the address to Lucien Bisset."

"Then what?" Mac asked.

"I thought I was done, but then they wanted me to get her DNA."

"My DNA? Why?" Roxanne asked.

"Ms. Harvey, you're not Conrad Harvey's bio-logical daughter. Your real father is Jean Laurent."

Roxanne let out a sarcastic giggle. "Bullshit," she said. "Jean Laurent?"

"I got your DNA from a napkin and fork you used at the Marriott. It was the same day I got the pictures of you two, the same picture they're showing on TV. You were swimming. McCaffrey walked away from the bar. I gave the napkin and fork to Bisset. He sent it for testing. I have a copy of the results in my car, or I can bring them up on my phone if you don't believe me. Your DNA is a 98.4 percent pater-nal match with Jean Laurent."

Roxanne sat down in a chair next to the bed. Mac put his hand on her shoulder.

"Well, who's Jean Laurent?" Hanrahan asked, breaking the silence. "Am I the only one still curious?"

"All I know is that he's a chef in Paris. How he knocked up your mother, I couldn't tell you. If you want more information, talk to Bisset. My job was to find you and get a DNA sample. That's it."

"Why did you sell your pictures to the *Enquirer*?" Mac asked.

"Money. They paid me five thousand dollars."

"You just called them on a whim?"

"No. Your editor in Aspen called me. Peril. He said you knew I was following Roxanne. Said he had a deal worked out with somebody at the *Enquirer* and asked if I wanted in."

"What a piece of shit," Mac said.

"I told you so," Hanrahan said. "Pissy little Davey Peril. I never liked that bitch."

"Which reminds me," Stransky said. "I have a deal for you, Ms. Harvey. Some business to discuss."

Stransky tried to sit up and straighten out. He was obviously in pain.

"What's that?" Roxanne asked.

"I'm prepared to tell the tabloids that Conrad Harvey wasn't your father. If they're willing to go page 1 with photographs of you drinking with this asshole, a 'who's your daddy' story could be worth a lot of money to a guy like me. Probably more than I got for the photos."

"You're a lowlife, Stransky," Mac said.

"I prefer opportunist."

Roxanne stood up and gazed out the window for a moment. Then she walked out of the room. Hanrahan followed her.

Mac asked, "What do you want?"

"Twenty-five thousand dollars."

"For what?"

"To not tell the *National Enquirer* that your girlfriend isn't related to Conrad Harvey. To not tell them her mom was a whore with a thing for Frenchmen and Roxanne is a love child."

"And you think that's worth twenty-five thousand dollars? Get real. You know nothing about publishing."

"I know your girlfriend doesn't want the attention. Am I right? Do you think Roxanne wants to stay in the tabloids? Do you think she wants her family name dragged through the mud? Her father just died, and now this? I want money, McCaffrey, and she's got the bread. That's the least she can do."

"What the fuck is it with this town and blackmail? First the cops, and now you?"

"It's catch and kill, McCaffrey. You pay me, and the story dies with me. You don't pay me, I sell my information to the tabloids. It's up to her."

"You're a real piece of work, you know that?" said Mac. "You just told this bereaved girl the man that raised her isn't her real father, and now you're trying to profit off of that?"

"Have you looked at me? She hit me with a fucking car!"

"And it's too bad she didn't kill you."

"Twenty-five thousand dollars is beer money to her. Wait until I talk to my lawyer. You can't go around running people over. I'm gonna sue her for a lot more than twenty-five thousand dollars. This is just the beginning of my windfall."

"Good luck with that. Cops already agreed it was self-defense. You have no case. Besides, what's your record look like up in Jersey?"

"My record in Jersey? What are you talking about?"

"You said it yourself. Twenty-five thousand dollars is nothing to Roxanne. What do you think she's willing to spend on legal defense if you come after her? You think you'll beat her in court? Her lawyers will eat you up. You'll probably lose your investigator license. You'll be finished."

"Yeah, well, maybe I'll take my chances," Stransky said.

"I guess everyone deserves a day in court."

"Get outta my room. Go talk to your girlfriend and tell her about my proposition."

"You have no cards to play." Mac got up to leave. "Fuck you, Stransky."

*****

Hanrahan drove Mac and Roxanne to the impound lot to pick up her Maserati, which now featured a pretty nice ding in the bumper. Mac called the car rental agency and told them where they could pick up the Mustang. He wasn't sure if it was the girl with the earring that had rented the car, but whoever he spoke with didn't sound real pleased about their vehicle being in an impound lot.

Mac tossed the keys onto the driver's seat and left it at that. He was bummed about giving up the convertible, but with no more expense account, they were gonna come looking for it anyway, he figured. Might as well let them pay to get it out of impound.

The three of them drove back to Roxanne's place on the beach, where Mac finally had a moment to return some phone calls. He stepped outside and dialed Charlie's cell phone while Roxanne laid down and Hanrahan got busy shaking himself up a martini. He was looking for olives when Charlie answered his cell phone.

"Have you seen the fucking news?"

"Uh, yeah, Charlie."

"You're on the cover of the *National Enquirer!*"

"Yes, I know."

"They're showing you and the Harvey broad together on TV!"

"I know."

"I told you, kid. I told you not to mess with her. Now you're both in the papers. The shitty papers too."

"Charlie, do you know how my photograph ended up on the cover of the *National Enquirer?*"

"Yeah, because you fucked the Harvey girl," Charlie said.

"Peril sold it to them."

Charlie paused. "He did? How do you know that?"

"He told me. He said he used the money to cover my expenses."

"You're kidding me."

"I'm not. Peril sold the story. He sold me out, Charlie."

"And the publishers were fine with that? Selling photo inventory to a tabloid?"

"That's what he said."

"What a prick."

Mac asked, "You had no idea? You didn't know about this?"

"Of course not. I have nothing to do with the budget. You know that."

"Peril didn't tell you he was selling the photographs?"

"No."

"Roxanne is pissed off," Mac said.

"What are you still doing out there? Get back to Colorado."

"What am I supposed to do? Peril cut the expense account. I got nowhere else to go, Charlie. I don't think I'm coming back. I think I'm gonna stick around here for a while."

"In Florida?"

"I like Florida."

"You're not coming back to Aspen?"

"Not anytime soon."

"What are you gonna do out there?"

"I think I might have lined something up at the *Palm Beach Post*."

"That's a good paper, Mac. You gonna cover local bands, live music?"

"I think I'm done with that beat. This is a news gig."

"News, huh? That's fantastic, kid. That's what you wanted. You'll see more action in Florida anyway. News desk is dead in this one-pony town."

"Charlie," Mac said. "You really should think about retiring. Get someplace warm already."

"I like Aspen," Charlie said. "Been here thirty years."

"Do you really want to keep working for Peril?"

"He's not the first asshole to run this paper. Besides, what else am I gonna do? I got ink in my blood, kid, just like you. But I'm too old to catch on anywhere else."

"You didn't save your money, did you?"

"Hell no. Do you know any fucking reporters that saved their money?"

"Maybe when I get my ducks in a row down here, you and Delores can come visit."

"Maybe. I dunno if her fat ass can fit on a plane anymore. It's been a while."

"Charlie…"

"Yeah?"

"You're a good editor. And a good friend."

"You ain't so bad either, kid. Good luck down there. Call me when you pass back through the Rockies."

"First one is on you."

"Fuck that," Charlie said. "I still have my expense account. First one is on the *Aspen Daily News*."

MONDAY

Hanrahan had already left when Mac woke up. He slipped out from under the covers and walked into Roxanne's kitchen to make coffee. He selected a coffee mug from the cabinet that was adorned with horses. He clicked on the yellow Moccamaster drip coffee pot.

The smell of brewing coffee woke Roxanne. She rolled from the bed and went to the bathroom. Mac poured a cup of coffee and smelled the half-and-half in the fridge.

"You want coffee?" he yelled across the flat.

"Yes, please. How's the creamer?"

Mac wasn't that confident. He took a second whiff. "It's fine," he said.

Mac poured two cups of coffee and splashed them with questionable creamer. Roxanne put on some music. It sounded like Joy Division, but maybe it was New Order. It was definitely English post-punk.

"Good morning," Mac said. "You sleep okay?"

"Not really, Mac. I've got a lot on my mind."

Roxanne rubbed her fingers through her hair. Mac handed her a cup of coffee. She flopped down on the love seat.

Mac asked, "Do you want to go see this Bisset guy? The lawyer Stransky was talking about?"

"We can start there." Roxanne took a sip of her coffee. "Thank you," she said.

"His office is in Palm Beach. I already looked up the address."

"Okay."

"Can I ask you something personal?" Mac said.

Roxanne said, "Of course."

"Do you believe all of this? Did you have any idea Conrad wasn't your real father?"

"I never thought about it before. I never had a reason to. He was never affectionate toward me though. If I really think about it, I guess I can see how I was more of his responsibility than anything else."

"Are you okay?"

"I'm a big girl."

"I'm not asking you if you're a big girl. I know that, but this is heavy shit. I'm just letting you know I care."

"I'm fine. Let's just go see what the lawyer has to tell us."

Mac dumped the rest of his coffee in the sink and got ready for a shower. Roxanne joined him.

*****

The law offices of Walker, Bisset, and Turnhill was located on the eighteenth floor of a sky rise off Clematis Street in West Palm Beach. The lobby window faced east. Mac noticed The Breakers off in the distance, the hotel where he and Roxanne had met Hanrahan a couple of days earlier. It seemed like much longer ago.

Roxanne approached a perky receptionist wearing glasses.

"Hello, I'd like to see Lucien Bisset," she said.

"Do you have an appointment?"

"Is he available?"

"Do you have an appointment?"

Mac interjected. "Is he in the goddamn building?"

"Excuse me?" said the receptionist.

"My name is Roxanne Harvey. Tell him it's me. And no, I don't have an appointment."

Roxanne slapped at Mac and gave him a dirty look. The receptionist picked up the phone.

"You get more bees with honey, you know," Roxanne said to Mac.

"There is a Roxanne Harvey here, Mr. Bisset," the receptionist said into the phone. "And she doesn't have an appointment."

She looked up at Mac. "She's got a man with her too," she said.

Mac smiled at the receptionist. She didn't smile back. Suddenly, a man appeared in the hallway beside the reception desk. He was wearing suspenders and black-framed eyeglasses.

"Hello, Ms. Harvey," he said. "And hello to you, Mr. McCaffrey."

"How do you know who I am?" Mac asked.

Bisset ignored the question. "I'm Lucien Bisset. Come back to my office, please."

Roxanne walked past the reception desk. Mac followed, stopping to snatch a lollipop from a jar on the receptionist's desk. He winked at her and she flashed a disapproving frown.

Bisset's corner office was large and plush. He had an enormous framed photograph of the Eiffel Tower on the south wall. He motioned for Mac and Roxanne to sit, and he slipped behind his desk and sunk into an enormous red leather chair.

"It's nice to finally meet you, Ms. Harvey," he said. "Where would you like to begin?"

"Where are my options?"

"I spoke to my private investigator this morning from the hospital."

"Are you his lawyer or employer?" Mac asked.

"Employer," Bisset said. "We don't represent Mr. Stransky in any legal manner."

"Why did you hire him to follow her?"

"I would prefer to answer Ms. Harvey's questions, Mr. McCaffrey."

"Then please do. And you can call me Mac."

"Mr. Bisset," said Roxanne, "your investigator told me yesterday that Conrad Harvey isn't my biological father. Is that true?"

"That is correct."

"How do you know this?"

"Did Mr. Stransky mention the DNA test results?"

"He did. But I'm still a little confused."

Mac took the lollipop out of his mouth, making a deliberate popping noise. "Come on, Frenchie, who is Jean Laurent?" he asked.

Bisset continued, "This office has a sister firm in Paris. About three weeks ago, Mr. Laurent walked into that office and had quite a story to tell. Would you like to hear it?"

"What the fuck do you think?" Mac asked.

Roxanne gave Mac an aggressive glance. "Yes, Mr. Bisset. I'd like to find out exactly what is going on. Who is my father, and why did you hire a private investigator to follow me?"

"And why are we both on the cover of the *National Enquirer*?" Mac said.

"Mr. Laurent walked into our Paris office about three weeks ago. This was shortly after your father, Conrad Harvey, passed away. Your adoptive father, Conrad Harvey, I should say."

"I'm not adopted," Roxanne said. "There are no amendments on my birth certificate. My parents are listed as Conrad Harvey and Suzette Cox. They both signed the certificate the day of my birth. I know this as fact."

"According to Mr. Laurent, he was a personal chef at the Harvey estate in Beverly Hills from 1979 until 1984. I have the address of the residence if you need it."

"I remember the house in Beverly Hills," Roxanne said.

Bisset pulled some documents from a drawer and slid them across the desk. "He has pay stubs and tax returns to prove that he worked and resided there."

Roxanne picked up the papers and glanced them over. "We had a rather large staff at that house," she said. "We always had a personal chef. We always had a kitchen staff. Neither of my parents were gifted in the culinary arts."

Bisset continued, "According to Mr. Laurent, he was a little more than just your mother's personal chef. He was also her lover. Apparently, for several years. He told us that when your mother became pregnant, he asked that she tell Conrad the child was his. However, and I have no reason to believe you would know this, but Conrad Harvey was sterile. He was unable to produce quality sperm. There was no way to suggest he was the father."

"My father couldn't have children?" Roxanne asked.

"Conrad Harvey could not have children, no, Ms. Harvey."

"So this man, Jean Laurent, is my biological father?"

"Yes, he is indeed," Bisset said.

"Why didn't they tell me this? Why didn't my parents tell me?"

"Mr. Laurent said that your mother, Suzette, desperately wanted children. When she found out she was pregnant, there was no way she was going to terminate what was likely her only chance to have a child. Conrad wasn't exactly thrilled with the situation, but he, too, was eager for a family he never thought he would have. They made the decision to raise you together. They both appear to have adored you, Ms. Harvey."

"What happened after she was born?" Mac asked. "Where did Laurent go?"

"When Conrad found out about the affair, he was initially livid, from what I am told. And I am old enough to remember watching your mother on television, and I could see why sharing her with another man wasn't high on Conrad's pleasure list," Bisset said. "They forced Mr. Laurent to sign a non-disclosure agreement. He was to never contact you. Ever. Conrad also pulled some strings to have Mr. Laurent's immigration status revoked, and he was deported back to France a few weeks before your birth. He has never been back to the United States, Ms. Harvey. He has never seen you in person."

Roxanne continued shuffling through the paperwork. "What does he do now? Where is he? Do I have siblings?"

"Jean Laurent owns a rather successful catering business in the Montmartre district in Paris. And yes, you have both a brother and a sister. Half-siblings, of course."

Roxanne sat back in her chair and looked over at Mac.

"This is crazy," she said. "I've been to Paris a dozen times."

"I hope you didn't fuck anyone named Laurent," Mac said.

Bisset slid more documents across his desk toward Roxanne. "The nondisclosure was very convincing to Mr. Laurent. He made no attempts to contact you, and he honored the contract," Bisset said.

"This may seem obvious," Mac said, "but why now?"

"He, as well as the rest of the world, saw the news that Conrad Harvey had died. With Suzette also being deceased, he contacted our office in Paris to see if the nondisclosure was still valid."

"Is it?" Roxanne asked.

"There is nothing Conrad can do to my client from the grave, Ms. Harvey. The nondisclosure was void as soon as your father died."

"Adoptive father," Mac said.

"Actually, there was no formal adoption," Bisset said. "Conrad and Suzette both went to the hospital together when she went into labor, and there was no mention at all of Jean Laurent. As far at the state of California is concerned, there was no adoption."

"This firm handles estates, is that correct?" Roxanne asked.

"Indeed."

"So what does Laurent want? What does my father want?"

"What are you implying, Ms. Harvey?"

"What do you think?" Mac said. "You know how much money Conrad Harvey was worth. Is this stinky Frenchman looking for a payout?"

"That's not exactly how I would have phrased it," Roxanne said. "But yes, is he looking for money?"

"I can assure you he is not, Ms. Harvey. My client has been waiting for over thirty years to be able to contact you. He has lived these last three decades watching from afar and wondering if there would ever be an opportunity for him to meet his firstborn."

Roxanne continued sifting through the paperwork Bisset had laid out in front of her.

"In that paperwork, you will find all the legalities. The nondisclosure, the termination paperwork, and a copy of the postmarked check your father gave Mr. Laurent when he dropped him off at LAX."

"What postmarked check?" Mac asked.

"In an effort to keep my client at a distance, Conrad gave him a check for two hundred thousand dollars that was dated on your birthday, Ms. Harvey. He presented him with the check before Mr. Laurent boarded his return flight to France. This was a payoff."

"That was a good chunk of change in the eighties," Mac said.

"Indeed. However, Mr. Laurent never cashed the check."

"Really?" Roxanne said. "Why not?"

"I told you, Ms. Harvey. Jean Laurent isn't interested in any money from the Harvey estate. He didn't want it then, and he doesn't want it now."

Bisset reached back into his desk drawer and retrieved two more envelopes. One appeared older and more weathered than the other. He handed them across the table.

"These are two letters addressed to you from Jean Laurent," Bisset said. "The first letter was written to you on the day of your birth. The second letter is much more recent and contains his current contact information. I don't suggest you read them now."

Roxanne tucked the letters into her bag.

"Is there anything else you would like to know, Ms. Harvey? Do you have any more questions?"

Roxanne pondered a moment and looked at Mac. She then glanced out the window briefly and let out a soft sigh. Mac put his hand on the back of her neck.

"I have a question," he said. "Why'd you hire a scumbag like Eli Stransky, and why are we on the cover of a supermarket tabloid?"

"Stransky is on retainer with this firm. We use him on locates. We sent somebody out to the Harvey Ranch in Wellington, but we had no luck finding you, Ms. Harvey. We engaged Stransky's services to find you so we could present you with these letters from your father."

"You know he's selling information on Roxanne? He sold those photographs," Mac said. "He's trying to profit off this."

"As I said, Mr. Stransky is on retainer with this firm. He's not on staff. He's free to make his money outside of our employ. I don't pay attention to his side hustles. Besides, I don't think he'll be following either of you anymore. He won't be walking anytime soon, from what I have been told. His leg is broken."

"He's still blackmailing her," Mac said.

"How so?" Bisset asked.

"He said he's going to tell the *National Enquirer* that Conrad wasn't my real father," Roxanne said. "He's going to keep selling stories about it."

Mac said, "It's checkbook journalism."

"I'm afraid that isn't something I can help you with," Bisset said. "I'm afraid that's between you, Mr. Stransky, and the *National Enquirer*. Ms. Harvey, do you have any other questions?"

"Yes, I do. Did he love my mother, Mr. Bisset? Did my real father love my mom, or was it just an affair?"

"When you are ready to read those letters, Ms. Harvey, I think your questions will be answered quite favorably."

*****

Mac snatched another lollipop on the way past the reception desk and winked again at the secretary, who glared at him like he just shit in her Cheerios.

Roxanne was in a bit of a daze when the elevator opened, and they stepped in.

"I think I want a drink," she said.

Mac looked at his watch as if it mattered. "I saw The Breakers from Bisset's window. You want to go see if Hanrahan is there? Maybe find out what's going on with the Deaver brothers, find out if there's a follow-up story coming?"

"That's fine," Roxanne said. She tossed her keys to Mac. "You drive."

Stepping off the elevator and crossing the lobby, Mac stopped Roxanne, grabbing her hand.

"Are you okay?" he asked. "I can't imagine how you feel."

"I'm used to it," she said.

"Used to what?"

"I'm used to people not knowing how I feel. My mother died when I was ten years old. Of a drug overdose. My family has always been under media scrutiny. I didn't grow up like you, Mac. My life was different."

"I never said it wasn't. I'm just asking if you're all right."

"What do you think?"

"Clearly, I think you might have some daddy issues now."

"Piss off."

"I'm joking. But honestly, I think Conrad Harvey provided you a fantastic life, financial freedom, and independence. I never met the man, but I have no doubt he loved you. You were his daughter. He raised you."

Mac and Roxanne walked out of the building and into the sunlight. Roxanne slipped on her over-sized designer shades. Mac put his shades on as well.

"Seems like quite the burden, though, right?" said Roxanne. "He went to his grave never telling me the truth. You don't think that's a little fucked up?"

"He was protecting his family."

"How so?"

"He loved your mother, right?"

"I don't know. She was a trophy wife. I'm sure he loved the idea of her."

"My guess is he never told you because he didn't want the information to ever get out. It would have made your mother look bad. It wouldn't have been a good look for the whole family. You know, extramarital affair. Rich television producer, trophy wife, mistress, love child. He probably didn't want that for you."

"He didn't want my mom to be labeled a whore?"

"Not a whore. Maybe *whorish*."

"I guess," Roxanne said. "I still feel sad for him. And now Stransky is going to leak it anyway. It's going to come out in the press all these years later."

"It hasn't happened yet. You have options."

"I'm not giving that guy twenty-five thousand dollars."

"Maybe we can kill the story before it leaks."

"You're pretty good at getting stories killed, right? Like your *Aspen Daily News* scoop?"

"I didn't kill that story on purpose. I just gave it to the *Post* instead."

"Your Aspen angle was bullshit anyway," Roxanne said. "Let's just go see Pat."

Mac steered Roxanne's Maserati over the Flagler Memorial Bridge and onto Royal Poinciana Way before turning again onto Breakers Row. The towering hotel was just as magnificent as the first time he had seen it.

He tossed the keys to a valet as a second one opened the passenger door.

"Hello, Ms. Harvey," the valet said.

"Hello," Roxanne said. "Have we met?"

"No. I saw you on television yesterday," the valet said. "You were leaving a courthouse in Delray Beach."

"Oh," Roxanne said. "Is that right?"

The valet closed the car door behind Roxanne. "You're all over the news, Ms. Harvey," he said. "It's kind of a big deal. People are talking about it on the island."

Mac walked behind the Maserati, locked arms with Roxanne, and whisked her into the lobby. He felt the stares as soon as she did.

"Are these people staring at me?" Roxanne asked.

They continued walking toward the seafood bar located in the back of the hotel.

"I think so," Mac said. "Who knew the tabloids had such an upper-crust readership?"

"The valet said I was on the news."

Mac continued ushering Roxanne toward the back bar. "I heard. Let's just get a drink," he said.

As expected, Hanrahan was seated at the seafood bar when Mac and Roxanne walked in. He was wearing a yellow linen suit and a powder-blue dress shirt. He eyeballed the two of them as soon as they entered the room.

"Oh, look, it's my tabloid babies!" he shrieked.

"You can probably stop calling us that now," Mac said.

"Why? I just saw the issue in the gift shop of this exact hotel. I even bought a copy."

Hanrahan tossed a copy of the *Enquirer* onto his copy of the *New York Post*, which rested on top of his copy of the *Palm Beach Post*. He spilled a little of his martini onto the bar. Mac looked at the tabloid.

"You really read this shit?"

"If you cover society and you don't read the tabloids, do you really cover society?" he said.

"At least you look hot, Roxanne. I look like a fucking albino," Mac said.

"I don't care about that. Pat, what's going on in Delray?" Roxanne asked, changing the subject. "Are the Deavers getting charged?"

"I thought you'd never ask. We got a press release this morning. Detective Deaver has been terminated without pay. The investigation is being turned over to the FBI, and the IRS is looking at tax records on the halfway houses."

"Holy shit, the feds?" Mac said.

"Delray PD wants to wash their hands of it. They're saying Deaver was just one bad egg in an otherwise sterling department. Sacrificial lamb. They're hanging him out."

KEVIN LYNCH

Mac slapped Roxanne on the ass. "That's fucking fantastic."

"What about his brother?" Roxanne asked. "He's the one that was dating Juliette."

"There was nothing in the press release about him, honey. But I'm sure he's being investigated."

"Are you following up?" Mac asked.

"Am I following up? That's your beat, Bernard."

"My beat?"

"Yes. I talked to the managing editor. There's a staff job at the *Palm Beach Post* if you want it. You can cover courts and crime in Delray Beach and Boca Raton."

"This is a staff job? Full time?" Mac asked.

"Yes, indeed, my dear. You just have to go through HR. The news desk was impressed with our story. My glowing recommendation didn't hurt either."

Mac was speechless. Roxanne slapped his ass. "That's fucking fantastic," she said.

Hanrahan said, "Aren't you two something cute?"

"What's the follow-up?" Mac asked. "Is there a deadline?"

"We're running with the press release tomorrow. After that, we'll wait for the federal investigation and pick it up there."

"Have the halfway houses been vacated?"

"That I couldn't tell you."

Roxanne ordered her complicated margarita and a Heineken for Mac.

"So, Roxanne," Hanrahan said. "Who's your daddy?"

"Excuse me?"

"Spill it, sister. I was in that hospital room yesterday. Who's the French fella?"

Roxanne licked the salt off the rim of her glass. "Apparently my mom had an affair with her chef in 1983. He's my biological."

"Conrad Harvey is not your father? This is scandalous, honey. So scandalous," Hanrahan said.

"Keep it down, Pat," Mac said. "She's not broadcasting it."

Hanrahan faked a zipper across his lips. "It won't be in my column," he said.

"It's going to get broadcasted soon enough," Roxanne said. "I'm not paying Stransky off, and he's still talking to the *Enquirer*."

She flipped the *Enquirer* over to avoid looking at herself.

"I might be able to help you there," Hanrahan said.

"How so?"

"I know a gal at the *National Enquirer*. She's a senior editor. Julia Baker. She's been there for thirty years. She was around when the paper was still running out of Lantana."

"Of course you do," Roxanne said. "You know everyone. You always have a source, Pat."

"And I have a secret to boot," Hanrahan said. "I have a chatterbox at Mar-a-Lago telling me Donald Trump is running for president next year."

"Bullshit," Mac said. "Donald Trump? 'The Apprentice' Donald Trump? That's laughable."

"No bullshit, Bernard. He's doing it."

"There's no way he's getting elected president. He won't even get the nomination," Roxanne said. "Not in this state, anyway. I thought Jeb was running."

"I don't even know what affiliation he is," Mac said. "Wasn't he a Democrat? I thought he hung around the Clintons."

"All that is trivial. It doesn't matter. It's a vanity project, honey. I have it on good authority he's running. And…I have a dumpster full of Trump stories for the tabloids. A bursting trove of scandal. The *Post* has been paying my membership at Mar-a-Lago for the last two decades. I have more dirt on Donald than anyone. It's no secret he's an adulterer, that's hardly news, but the list of partners is juicy. There's even a porn star I can get on record. I also know he's paid hush money to a Playboy model. And the Epstein parties? You can't fathom *that* level of debauchery and decadence."

"How does this help Roxanne?" Mac asked.

"I think the *National Enquirer* would be far more interested in running stories about Donald Trump than stories about Conrad Harvey's little girl. No offense, Roxy."

"None taken," Roxanne said. She took a sip of her margarita. Her lipstick left a smudge on the glass where the salt had previously been.

"Julia and I have a history of covering Donald Trump. I was their source during the Marla Maples affair all the way up until their divorce," Hanrahan said.

Mac asked, "You sold gossip to the tabloids?"

"Of course, I did. How do you think I afforded all those trips to New York and Aspen? Trump was a gold mine back then. Now that he's running for president, I shall return to the well, so to speak."

"How is this going to keep them from running any more stories about Roxanne and her father?"

Hanrahan continued, "I'll have them agree to kill any and all stories about Conrad and Roxanne in exchange for exclusive Donald Trump gossip. I can feed them page 1s for weeks. In a couple of months, they won't care about Conrad Harvey anymore. Trump will dominate the news cycle as soon as he enters the race."

Hanrahan tilted back the last of his martini and started working on a spear of olives.

"You think they'll go for that?" Mac asked.

"Of course, darling."

"That's unbelievable, Pat."

"Yes, I am rather unbelievable."

"You're going to provide gossip on Donald Trump to the *National Enquirer*, and in exchange, they're going to kill any stories about Roxanne and her family?"

"Yes, Bernard. That's the plan."

"And I have a staff job at the *Palm Beach Post*?"

"That too."

Mac took a sip of his Heineken and waved to the bartender. "What a week," he said. "Does anyone else want a shot? How's the expense account at the *Post* anyway?"

*****

After devouring an early lunch of margaritas, beers, whiskey, oysters, shrimp, and stone crab, Mac and Roxanne bid farewell to Hanrahan and escaped Palm Beach in her car, heading south on A1A back toward Delray Beach. Roxanne seemed in good spirits despite the earlier events of the day. Maybe it was the booze, Mac thought.

"What do you want to listen to?" Roxanne asked while messing with the stereo.

"I dunno," Mac said. "You pick."

Roxanne put on something that sounded great coming through the Ghibli speakers. The bass was loud. It sounded like Southern California surf punk. Probably Pennywise.

She bobbed her head for a while before dropping the sun visor and glossing her lips with pink lipstick.

"Where are we going?" Mac asked. "You making yourself pretty?"

"I want to go back to the marina where Deaver docks his boat," Roxanne said. "Boynton Harbor Marina." She smacked her lips together and flipped the visor back up.

"*The Takedown*?"

"Yeah, the charter boat."

"Why? You think that's a good idea? The half-way houses are closed, Roxanne. The Deaver brothers are out of business."

"I just wanna see if he's still taking girls out on the boat. Those girls probably got evicted."

"I'm sure the feds have tied up all business assets. The boat might be evidence at this point. They may have even seized the boat."

"Just because the halfway houses are closed doesn't mean he's not still plundering meetings and pushing girls off the wagon. He could still be selling patients to other junkie hunters."

"While he's under investigation? Doesn't sound likely."

Roxanne rolled her window down, leaned her seat back, and stuck her feet out over the side mirror. Her toenail polish matched her lipstick.

"I want to ask him about Juliette," Roxanne said. "I need to know if he feels bad about it. If he's sorry."

"You want an apology from this guy? Doesn't sound like a good idea."

"Not an apology. More like a confession. You got your story and a job out of this, Where's my satisfaction? I feel like some comeuppance for this asshole is in order, don't you?"

"His brother got fired from the police department, and they're losing millions in income. They both might go to jail," Mac said.

"I was looking for Diver before I even met you. I was going trolling drug and alcohol meetings to find him. And now you think it's over for me?"

Mac could tell she was serious. "I'll do whatever you want."

"Let's just go see if the boat is there."

The car continued south on A1A, passing the Dune Deck where Mac had initiated contact with Roxanne only a few days prior. Mac nodded toward the parking lot.

"Too bad we already ate," he said. "Do you wanna stop for a drink?"

"We can get a drink over by the marina."

"Do you need to stop by your place? We're gonna drive right past it."

"No, I don't need to stop. Why? Do you want to change shirts?"

Mac looked at his attire. "What's wrong with this one? Are you laughing at my look again? I got this from the Target in Glenwood Springs."

Roxanne giggled. "I can't believe you wear flip-flops and Hawaiian shirts in Aspen."

"You don't see the satire in that?"

"Of course, I do." She giggled again.

Mac asked, "Are you drunk?"

"I didn't eat much."

"Tequila on an empty stomach," Mac said. "This oughta be fun."

Driving past the Sun Dek, Mac noticed an inappropriate number of vehicles parked in the adjacent guest parking lot. Roxanne noticed too.

"You've got company," Mac said.

"Who is that?"

There was a television news van parked on Inlet Cay Drive. Mac kept driving.

Roxanne cocked her head back. "Was that a news van?" she asked. "How do they know where I'm staying?"

"Stransky," Mac said.

"Why do they care? I'm not famous."

"Your dad was. So was your mother."

"I'm not."

"You sell papers."

"Why?"

"Cult of celebrity."

"How so?"

"Celebrity is tied to consumer interests, and selling newspapers is exactly that. Celebrity culture is fashion and image. Andy Warhol's whole career was based on this. Look at Edie Sedgwick. She had no discernible talents, and Warhol made her a star."

"Are you saying I have no discernible talents? You sure know how to sweet-talk a girl."

"That's not what I mean. Sedgwick was a socialite. She happened to be gorgeous, and as a matter of fact, you look a lot like her."

"That's slightly more flattering."

"You're a bombshell. A rich bombshell," Mac said. "You look good on magazine covers. Image sells over substance in the tabloid press. Any day."

"I don't want the attention, Mac. I don't want any of this."

"Hanrahan said he can kill it," Mac said.

"That wasn't just the tabloid press back there. That looked like a lot of people."

"It will blow over. Warhol said everyone gets fifteen minutes of fame. Hopefully for you, it's only fifteen minutes. Maybe it will be less."

"Wasn't Andy Warhol high on drugs when he said that?"

"Extremely," Mac said. "He painted Campbell's Soup cans. Do you know how high you gotta be to paint fucking soup cans? But he did understand celebrity."

"I'll be happy when this is all over," Roxanne said.

*****

Boynton Harbor Marina was somewhat empty for a Monday. A small lunch crowd was seated at the Two Georges tiki bar, but only a few boats remained docked in the waterway. Instead of parking in the garage, Mac found a place to parallel park in front of the docked boats. Deaver's boat was a few yards away. There was a pickup truck backed up near it, and two guys were loading the flatbed with scuba gear taken off the boat. They had matching crew shirts that read "*The Takedown.*"

Mac motioned ahead of him. "There's Deaver's boat," he said.

Roxanne said back, "I see it."

They climbed out of the car and walked toward the boat. Darrin Deaver himself was seated at the steering column, texting on his phone. It became clear his two mates were cleaning out the boat, filling the truck with oxygen tanks and fishing rods.

"You guys doing tours today?" Roxanne asked.

Deaver looked up from his phone. "Tours?" he said.

"You going out on any charter trips?"

Deaver walked toward the stern of the boat and looked up at Roxanne. "No," he said. "Not today."

"What about tomorrow?"

"No."

"Isn't this a charter boat?" Roxanne asked.

"Yes, it is. But we're not taking people out for a few weeks," he said. "We're on hiatus."

"Why's that?" she asked.

Deaver lowered his sunglasses. The boat rested a few feet below dock level and he had to lift his head up to see Roxanne, who stood over him.

"Because," Deaver said. "We just are."

The two workers kept unloading gear from the boat. Mac took a flier for *The Takedown* from a plastic sleeve attached to a pilon. It was the same one he'd grabbed a couple of days earlier.

"Says here you sell diving and fishing tours," Mac said, reading from the flier.

Deaver shifted his eyes to Mac. "Normally we do," he said.

"Must be slow then," Mac said. "Isn't this kind of peak season?"

Deaver looked back and forth between Roxanne and Mac.

"Do I know you two or something?"

"I know your brother," Mac said.

"Do you?"

"Not very well. I know he's an asshole. Is that genetic?"

"What's that supposed to mean?"

"It means hereditary."

"Who are you?"

Roxanne cut back into the conversation. "Does the name Juliette Morgan mean anything to you?"

Deaver paused and ogled the leggy girl standing in front of him. "It doesn't mean much to me," he responded.

"That's the wrong answer," Mac said.

"Well, ask another question then. Seriously, do I fucking know you? How do you know my brother?"

"I met your brother a couple of days ago. He interviewed me about an accidental death. Maybe you heard about it. Guy in Delray Beach got hit by a train. Your brother tried to drum up a phony murder charge against me, so I helped expose his crooked business dealings in the rehab and recovery industry. Maybe you saw that article in the *Palm Beach*

Post. Maybe you're involved in it. Either way, I got him fired, and now he's under a federal investigation. Does any of this sound familiar, Darrin?"

Deaver paused. He was putting it together.

"I know who you are," he said. "You're that reporter. From Colorado, right?"

Deaver tried to step off the boat. Roxanne pushed him back with her foot. "Don't come up here," she said. "Stay there."

"Fuck you," Deaver said. He tried again to step up out of the boat. This time, Roxanne kicked him in the center of his chest. He stumbled back. The two workers stopped loading the truck and looked over at the commotion.

"You bitch," Deaver said.

"So I guess it is genetic after all," Mac said. "You're an asshole too."

"I'm gonna ask you again what you know about Juliette Morgan," Roxanne said.

"What do you want to know? She's dead. She was a junkie. She overdosed, and she's dead."

"You were her boyfriend," Roxanne said.

"That's news to me."

"She said you were her boyfriend."

"I think maybe a lot of girls think I'm their boy-friend, okay?"

"Did you get her hooked on drugs?"

"She was hooked on drugs before she met me. She was in recovery."

"She was sober when she met you. She had been clean for almost a year. Why did she relapse?"

"I don't know. She was a junkie. I'm getting off this boat. If you kick me again I'm gonna break your fucking ankle."

Deaver tried again to step up onto the dock. This time, Roxanne pulled a gun from her bag and leveled it at Deaver's face.

"I said stay on the boat," she said.

Deaver didn't move.

"Jesus Christ, Roxanne. What are you doing?" Mac said.

"Did you give drugs to Juliette?" Roxanne asked. "Did you get her to relapse?"

The two workers inched their way toward Roxanne. She turned and faced them. She pointed the gun at waist level.

"I will shoot you both in the dick," she said. They stopped moving. She put the gun back on Deaver.

"Where did you get that gun?" Mac asked. "Is that Stransky's gun?"

Roxanne didn't answer. She stared coldly at Deaver.

"Answer me," she said.

Deaver was frozen, standing still and contemplating how serious his current situation was. He looked around the marina. Nobody seemed to notice the pretty girl with the short blond hair pointing a gun in his face.

"I think I'd answer her," Mac said. "Did you hear what she said? She might shoot you in the dick.

I've never seen that before. It sounds like something maybe worth watching."

"I got Juliette into a halfway house," Deaver finally said.

"A halfway house you own?" Roxanne said back.

"Yeah, so what? She relapsed, and I had a bed at one of my halfway houses."

"But you're the one that got her to relapse in the first place. You got her to relapse so you could bill her insurance company. Answer me. Did you give drugs to Juliette?"

"I don't have to answer this shit. Call the cops," Deaver said.

"You mean like your brother?" Mac said. "Last time I saw him, he was being metaphorically butt-fucked by the FBI in an interrogation room down at the station."

"Fuck this," Deaver said. "I'll call the cops myself."

Deaver reached back for his cellphone, and Roxanne squeezed the trigger. The bullet ripped through the steering column of the boat.

"Whoooooooaaaaa, fuuuckkkk," Mac said.

The gunshot drew attention, the sound echoing loud off the water. Now everyone in the marina was looking in their direction. The tiki bar patrons all put down their piña coladas and mai tais.

"Just tell me," Roxanne said. "Did you give drugs to Juliette?"

"Yes," Deaver said. "I gave her drugs. Is that all you wanted to know, you crazy bitch?"

Roxanne emptied the clip into the ship deck with a series of deafening gunshots. Deaver hit the deck and crawled toward the bow of the boat. His two friends took off running before Roxanne had a chance to shoot them in the dick.

"We gotta go," Mac said. "We gotta go!"

The Takedown started sinking fast. Water was shooting up and out of the bullet holes like geysers. Deaver poked his head up from behind the steering column. He tried uselessly to stop one of the leaks.

"We really gotta go," Mac said.

Roxanne threw the pistol off the dock and into the water. Mac grabbed her hand and dragged her back to the Maserati. Mac sped through the valet and fishtailed out of the marina. Two employees jumped out of the way. The smell of burning rubber filled the air as Mac sped east over the bridge toward Ocean Boulevard. Mac looked down from the drawbridge just as *The Takedown* finished sinking in the brackish marina canal.

*****

"What's with the Bonnie and Clyde?" Mac asked. "You're running people over, stealing guns, and sinking boats now? You almost shot Deaver!"

Roxanne corrected him. "I didn't shoot anyone," she said.

"You know we're gonna get arrested, right? You do know what you pulled back there is…I don't know…I'm assuming at least felony vandalism."

Mac ran a red light, turning left onto A1A.

"Just go to my place," Roxanne said. "It's fine."

"Fine?" Mac said. "Fine? You just destroyed a hundred-dollar boat."

"I don't care about the money."

"Do you care about jail?"

Roxanne laughed. "I'm not going to jail."

Mac pulled into the Sun Dek, crashing into the parking block for unit number 5. The throng of press had already left. They ran upstairs. Roxanne flung a suitcase onto the bed and began tossing clothes into it. Mac watched her.

"What are you doing?"

"Pack your stuff," she said. "Whatever you have, just grab it."

Roxanne walked into the bathroom and came back with a toiletry bag.

"Where are we going?" Mac asked.

Roxanne stopped and looked up. "Dude, just get your shit together before the cops get here. The car is registered at the Wellington estate, but if those reporters that were camped out earlier found this address, you can be sure the police can get here pretty quickly too."

"My bags are already packed," Mac said. "I never unpacked after Key West."

Roxanne asked, "Do you have all your clothes?"

"My Hawaiian shirts and one pair of jeans? Yes. I didn't pack socks."

Roxanne looked around the room. She nodded toward the nightstand. "Don't forget your laptop.

And your phone charger." She clicked her luggage shut. "You ready?" she asked.

"Do you want to tell me what the hell that was all about?"

"What?"

"Your yippee-ki-yay motherfucker moment back there. Did you steal Stransky's gun?"

"It was in my car when we picked it up at impound."

"When did you decide to pretend Deaver's boat was Sonny Corleone?"

"It was reactionary. Come on, we gotta go."

"Reactionary?"

"I didn't plan it. It just sorta happened, Mac. Come on!"

"Just sorta happened?"

"Look, you got your revenge on Deaver number 1, I got mine on Deaver number 2. Let's just go. I'll drive."

"I didn't fly out here seeking revenge."

"You didn't fly out here to get in my pants either, but here we are."

Mac relented. "It was kinda sexy," he said.

"Really?"

"Yeah, you looked hot."

"Well, that's good because you looked like you shit your pants. Not the best look for you actually."

"Where are we going?" Mac asked again.

"Come on!"

Roxanne grabbed the keys from Mac's hand. They walked outside and she locked the door behind her. Mac dragged the suitcases and tossed them in the back of Roxanne's car. He climbed in shotgun as Roxanne was adjusting her seat. "Put your seat belt on," she said.

Roxanne gassed the car back onto A1A and started speeding south.

"What's the secret, Roxanne? Where are we going?"

Roxanne kept an eye on her rearview mirror as if she was anticipating the inevitable wail of police sirens.

"Miami," she said.

"What's in Miami?"

"The Miami International Airport."

"What's at the Miami International Airport?"

"Airplanes," she said. "And pilots."

"Are you gonna tell me where we're going or not?"

Roxanne asked, "Do you have a passport?"

*****

Mac was ashamed to admit it, but at thirty-three years old, he had never flown first class before. But he also felt it was worth the wait. The chair was heavy and white leather, and it reclined all the way back. His flip-flop–clad feet were practically staring right back at him. He even had his own flat-screen television, and the Nuggets were playing the Heat again. Mac had changed his clothes in the airport bathroom. He was wearing his powder-blue Hawaiian shirt, the one with the hula girls on it.

Once Roxanne had paid for the airline tickets, they were seated almost immediately. Mac wasn't sure if her paying cash expedited the boarding process or not, but he wasn't questioning it. He was just glad to be in the air before the police caught up to them. He even had a chance to phone Hanrahan before they took off to let him know he still wanted the job at the *Palm Beach Post*, but Roxanne needed to take care of some business first. Hanrahan was accommodating, and he let Mac know the gig would be waiting for him when he got back to Florida. There was no rush, he said.

The pilot came on the intercom to let everyone know they'd reached their cruising altitude of thirty-two thousand feet and were now free to walk around the cabin. Although Mac didn't feel like walking anywhere.

A pretty flight attendant approached their seats. She smelled like cinnamon and had perfect teeth. Her name tag read Tiffany.

"Good evening, Mr. McCaffrey," she began.

"Please call me Mac."

"Good evening, Mac. Would you like a drink menu?" she asked.

Mac rolled his head toward Roxanne. "Champagne?"

She nodded in approval.

"Do you have Dom Perignon on board, Tiffany?"

"Of course, Mr. McCaffrey."

"Mac."

"Of course, Mac."

"Great. Bring us a bottle of that on ice, of course."

"Of course."

"And I will also have a dirty Ketel One martini, straight up with one olive. Very cold, please."

"Will that be all?"

"And some Heinekens, please. I think four Heinekens should be good."

"Yes, sir. Would you like them on ice as well?"

"Of course."

"Anything else?"

"Please bring a food menu. I assume we have caviar and escargot?"

"*Oui*," Tiffany said. "We have a Kaluga and Paddlefish sampler that should pair well with the champagne."

Mac said, "Perfect."

Tiffany scuttled away with Mac's order. Roxanne lazily rolled her head toward him and smiled the way she did. The last sunshine of the day bounced around the first-class cabin and shone softly against her pale-blue eyes. "Are you sure that will be all, Mr. McCaffrey?" she joked. "Four beers, a martini, champagne, and caviar?"

"Why not?" he said. "We're only going as far as Paris. Oh, and please, Ms. Harvey, call me Mac."

The End

ABOUT THE AUTHOR

KEVIN LYNCH WAS RAISED IN Upstate New York. After graduating college in Colorado, he was hired as a staff reporter at the *National Enquirer,* where he traversed the country, making extended stops in Los Angeles, South Florida, and Las Vegas. He is currently settled in Palm Beach County, Florida, where he works as a private investigator and lives near the beach with his dog, Gonzo.

9 781646 549825